ReFoRMed

JUSTIN WEINBERGER

SCHOLASTIC INC.

For teachers who get it, and for kids who don't. You're pretty great.

TABLE OF CONTENTS

The Freak

Big gobs of summer have been splashing down on East Huron faster and faster. Ice-cream trucks, swimming pools, shouts from kids playing games out in the neighborhood after dinner— every gob is a meteor smashing into the ground just over the next hill, but still we have to pretend that we don't notice for two more days.

"Ian," says Mr. Dunford. "You want to read the next passage, please?"

"Um, what?" I say.

Giggles come from the girl behind me. *Don't turn around*, I tell myself. *Just ignore it . . .*

"Page four thousand eighty-seven, bottom paragraph," Mr. Dunford directs.

"Four *thousand*?"

"Bottom paragraph."

"My, uh—my book doesn't . . ." The giggles spread and I realize how gullible I am. "Oh . . . I get it."

"Ah," says the teacher. "Well then. There's hope for him yet."

I feel my cheeks getting redder.

"Ian, buddy, I know it's the end of the year. But if you want to go to Field Day tomorrow we need to finish strong, okay? Page twenty-one."

"Yes, Mr. Dunford."

I can feel everything in my guts tighten up as I try to read this passage about Thomas Edison.

Reading in class is one of my least favorite things to do. Oh, I can read like a fish can swim—but as soon as someone makes me do it out loud, it's a completely different thing. I just stammer and get embarrassed, which makes me stammer worse . . .

It's so much easier to get people to like you if you stay quiet and let them talk until you can figure out what they want to hear.

As I read about Thomas Edison, I wonder what he was like as a kid. He probably worked hard *all* the time, even if it was really nice out. Closed all the curtains and lit some candles, so he could fool himself into thinking it was cold and rainy and easier to concentrate on homework.

Maybe one day his candle went out and he didn't have any more and that's when an idea for a great new invention hit him.

A lightbulb sparked in his head, and then he yanked it right out of his imagination and all of a sudden it was real. Chainsaws, Sputnik, the Internet . . . all because this one kid focused on school, even though his friends were probably having a sleepover without him.

"Thomas Edison dropped out of school after only three weeks." The girl who giggled, Amy, picks up reading where I left off.

A murmur rolls around the room.

"Don't get excited," Mr. Dunford warns us. "Even though he didn't go to school he studied hard on his own. Very hard. Point is: For Thomas Edison to really get his brain going, he needed to find a personal *reason* to work hard."

Amy's hand goes up. "What was it?" she asks, like she's about to hear a secret trick to being smart.

"I don't know," says Mr. Dunford.

She deflates.

"More importantly, Amy, what engages *you*? What gets you excited to learn?"

Maybe we need to drop out of school and find out! I should say. Why can't I just raise my hand and do it?

"Everybody's passions are different," Mr. Dunford goes on. "Your job, guys, is to figure out what makes the world come alive for you. It's tricky, though. And it never gets easier. And sometimes it'll change, or you'll lose it for a while and then find it all over again . . ."

He trails off and waves his hands as if scattering a cloud of smoke. He does this a lot and I kinda like it.

"Anyway," he adds, "you won't believe me until you experience it yourself. Luckily, for one day longer you have to do whatever I tell you. So: This is your *homework assignment*. . . ." He pauses for the weary groans of complaint. "Stop. Your homework is a personal reflection. Tonight I want you to write about what you learned about yourself this past year—and try to remember that Thomas Edison was just like most of you. He was an indifferent student, right up until he wasn't."

"What's *indifferent* mean?" asks this kid Kyle.

"Who can define the word *indifferent*?" Mr. Dunford asks.

Just at that moment, the bell rings and thirty textbooks close with a ragged chain of *thwumps*.

"Yes, that's pretty much exactly what it means," Mr. Dunford mumbles to himself.

Chairs screech and somebody taps me on the back: "He's talking to *you*, Ian," says Amy.

"What?"

"You're indifferent. Like Thomas Edison. You gotta find something to care about."

She lifts her eyebrows like it's a dare, and I blink in confusion.

The girls I know are hard to figure out sometimes. I mean, on one hand, I'm pretty sure Amy's teasing me, but on the other? She just said I was like a young Thomas

Edison—which is basically calling me a genius. It's like, you know how *flammable* and *inflammable* both mean the same thing? Okay, well they totally do. They both mean "this thing loves to catch on fire!" except one doesn't take as long to say. Which is useful when things are on fire. Except if you're me. Because I'd be standing there in the middle of a burning building, staring at one thing labeled *flammable* and another labeled *inflammable* and get totally distracted trying to figure out why we have *two* words. I don't know why I'm even telling you that.

Oh yeah, because that's what it's like for me when I'm looking at Amy. The questions all bounce around inside my brain, and I just wind up staring like a freak, not saying anything.

Amy frowns. "I just meant—if you need any help with your reflections, I could help you."

"You think I can't figure out a dumb homework assignment?" I say. It comes out too loud.

She looks down, like *she's* the one who's embarrassed.

"I didn't mean it like that," I add.

"Whatever." She grabs her stuff to leave. "I was just trying to help."

Nice going, Freak, I tell the monster inside my head. It's always lurking there, and loves to do awkward things to ruin my life.

"If Ian Hart needs help with something, he knows better than to ask a know-it-all like you," another voice interrupts.

I feel an arm around my shoulder, and I smile up at my friend Devon Crawford as he pulls me away. Devon's like that—there when you need him, with just the right thing to say. He's always the cool one.

"See ya later, Lamey!" Devon calls over his shoulder.

Okay, sometimes he can be a bit of a jerk.

As I turn back toward Amy and see her face all clouded up, she spins away and I kinda feel bad.

Devon just looks at me. "What, do you like her or something?"

"Huh?" I say. "*No.*"

"Then forget about it. Dunford was talking to *you*, right?"

I nod.

"Yeah," he continues, "so it's none of her business. What's she doing butting in, telling you you're *indifferent*?"

"Yeah, you're probably right."

"I know I am," says Devon. "Plus? You're definitely different, dude."

"Uh huh?"

"And anyway, you've got *me*."

"Yeah, I know."

"Good thing too," he says. "Otherwise you would've fallen in, like, a well or something by now."

"Gimme a break," I say. "More like a volcano."

He grins. "Where would you even find a volcano around here?"

I open my mouth to answer but he cuts me off. "Okay, my bad. I totally believe you could find one, don't take it as a challenge or anything. Let's go find Mark and Ash."

I'm not sure whether to be hurt or flattered. So I shut up and follow.

Rules You Already Know

Devon paces down the aisle toward the back of the bus and plants his feet right in front of Max's seat, with that smile he gets when he's looking for trouble.

"What's up, Maxy?" he says. "You excited to get out there tomorrow?"

"What's tomorrow?" says Max.

"Field Day!" says Devon.

"Oh," Max says. "Yeah, not really."

"Aw, come on, Max," says Devon.

Here's the thing about Max Willis. He's exactly like me, only it's like no one ever told him the rules for being the new kid. You know the rules, right? They're not written down or anything, but everyone seems to just know them. First rule—

"Just don't forget to bring your inhaler," says Devon.

No, not that. I mean, for sure, if you *need* an inhaler, then yeah, but the first rule is—

"Don't forget to zip up your pants, bonehead," says Max.

Devon glances down at his pants and then back up at Max. His expression goes dark as he realizes he fell for the old made-ya-look.

This is not good. There's a feeling of pressure right in between my shoulders.

"Zip up my pants?" Devon says with a gleam in his eye. "Oh right—thanks for the reminder. I wouldn't want to lose them. Stuff around here seems to disappear ever since you moved in. I think it gets sucked up into your butt like a vacuum."

First rule is *BE QUIET AND FIT IN*, MAX.

And I'm not sure if it's because he can hear me screaming that warning at him inside my brain, but Max does get quiet. And then he notices the snip of laughter coming from Mark and the way Ash fidgets with his sleeves.

"Screw this," he says, shouldering past Devon.

"Where ya going, Maxy?" says Devon. "Hey! Don't worry. We'll have a Lost and Found for you. You just take your time removing all that stuff. Wash it with soap."

The busload of kids is like a pack of prairie dogs poking their heads over the seats to look at the new kid.

"What's going on back there?" the driver calls out, far too late to do any good.

"Nothing, Lisa," says Max, slumping into the seat behind her.

A glance passes between Max and Ash before Ash looks back down, embarrassed.

"See ya tomorrow, Ash," says Max.

Devon waves. "See ya tomorrow, Max!" he calls out in a big, cheerful voice.

I take the seat next to Ash, but he won't look at me. Even though we're best friends.

We've been best friends for, like, I don't know. Seven million years. I mean, ever since we tried to bike all over East Huron and explore everything we could in this boring town: the weird empty lots where nobody lives, the library at the top of the steepest hill in the known universe, the barn by the highway with the creepy tourist attractions from 1957 . . .

We didn't tell our moms about that last one, though, and after they found out, we weren't allowed out of the neighborhood anymore. Which only made us closer, since we were stuck circling the same block.

It's also the reason we agreed to play soccer with some kids from school one fateful day, even though we both knew we'd fail hard at it. And about seven seconds into the game someone who may or may not be named Ashley Darius Franklin kicked the ball and sent it *flying* into the neighbor's front window.

The whole glass pane spiderwebbed. Then half the neighborhood boys scattered as this *huge* guy in a robe slammed the door open . . . but Ash and I froze in fear as he marched toward us.

Which is how we met Devon.

No, not the guy in the robe. The kid standing in the doorway behind him. Hard to see right away, because we were focused on the goon hurling insults at us. Insults that would only make sense later, after a lot of googling. (About the googling, I will just say one thing, and that thing is: eew.) But that's Devon's older brother all right . . . super gross. He probably should've been locked up in the basement, if we were living in a more civilized world.

And then Devon stepped into the sunlight. "Colin, knock it off!"

He stood there on the porch with a phone in his hand, his thumb hovering over it like it was a detonator—

Colin straightened up like he was about to explode, but instead just stomped away, muttering something about Devon cleaning up the mess.

"What just *happened*?" I asked him.

"Well . . . you broke my house, dude," said Devon.

"I meant with *that* guy."

"Oh, my brother? Don't worry, I got blackmail on him. Just stick with me and he won't bother you."

And he was right.

Later, when Devon showed me his blackmail, I would learn that it was a really embarrassing video of that huge dude in the bathrobe breaking down and bawling when Devon's mom told him to "grow up" as she set fire to his favorite stuffed animal in their fireplace. I remember laughing, because that's what Devon was doing . . . but inside my head, there was a small voice that thought it was totally messed up. Back then, I could still tell that voice to shut up, though. Back then, in those simpler times, it wasn't a fully formed Freak.

A Little "Fun"

First thing the next morning it hits me: FIELD DAY! Pillows fall everywhere as I hurl myself out of bed and toward the unsuspecting world. And by unsuspecting world I mean my dog Scarlet, who gets excited by my sudden movement and lunges for me, tail wagging.

Scarlet gets excited whenever people around her are excited. Or when there's someone at the door. Or when there's nobody at the door, or when you brush your teeth, or when you spell out a word of a thing she's excited about. How does a dog know how to spell, you ask? She doesn't. She has to be excited *all* the time, just to be safe.

"Ian, come *on*!" Mom calls up the stairs to me.

"Coming . . ."

I pull on my jeans and a shirt, and my shoes make their way onto my feet by magic, I think. Or without help from my hands, at least. I stumble through the house and a series of crashes marks my progress, Scarlet the Blunderpup bouncing next to me all the way to the door.

In the distance, I see the bus turning the corner as I burst into the sunlight.

"Don't forget your lunch, Ian!" Mom calls.

"Crap." I turn on my heel and try to snag a brown paper bag off the counter, but I knock it on the ground and everything falls out.

"Gimme a *break*," I complain as I pick it up again.

Then I see the sludge inside.

"Peanut butter, Mom? It's my last day."

"And I hope you have a *good* one!" she says, holding open the door.

I run to the end of the block and the bus almost drives off, but I wave my arms like I'm stranded on a desert island and this is my one chance for rescue, and the driver takes pity and waits.

"Thanks, Lisa," I pant, barely able to speak I'm breathing so hard. She just shakes her head and drives off.

I plunk down next to Ash halfway back.

"You didn't do your reflection," he says. It's not a question.

I make a face. "Ehh. Can I copy yours?"

"No cheating. Anyway, it's the last day. I doubt Mr. Dunford will keep you inside."

"But he said—"

"Come on," he pleads. "I wanna do a puzzle. Did you bring it?"

I grin and open my backpack to pull out this creepy old

book we found in a creepy old bookshop—it's full of weird, impossible riddles. The sort of riddles that just might open up the door to some weird, impossible world, you know? Because books in old bookshops are usually magic.

I mean, even if this one isn't . . . there's a warning on the front that says *"This book will break your brain!"* and I'm never *not* going to investigate a claim like that. But joke's on you, book: can't break something that was born broken, so Ash and I are immune.

"Which one should we do?" Ash asks.

"You pick." I hand over the book.

He flips through and his eyes light up. "Okay. There's a dead body in the middle of a room. There's no way in or out—"

"Did it already."

"Without me?" says Ash.

I feel a pang of guilt. "You were there in spirit."

Ash frowns. "I didn't even read the whole thing. Are you sure you did it?"

"There's a puddle next to the body, right?"

"Lame," he says, heaving with disappointment. "All right, fine. What was the murder weapon?"

"I don't remember. The killer had a cool name, though. Had something to do with . . ."

A head pops up over the seat in front of us: "It was an icicle!" says Max. "He was stabbed with a knife made out of ice, and after he was stabbed, it melted."

Ash turns to me with a frown. "Well that would've been a fun one to figure out."

Max nods. "The murderer should be called *the ici-killer.*"

"You have this book too, Max?" asks Ash.

"I *love* that book," says Max.

Just then Lisa pulls up to the curb.

"Happy last day, kids!" she sings out. The brakes heave a pent-up breath of air and we push out of the bus in a big pile. But then the sight before us stops us in our tracks.

It's our own private amusement park.

Carnival games, popcorn, cotton candy, dunk tank, bean-bag toss, water balloons, prizes . . . and it's all untouched. Just waiting for us.

"Field Day," says Ash in a half whisper.

Max's eyes get big too. "We never had this at my old school."

A car horn honks behind us just as a woman bellows, "You call this an education?"

We turn in time to see Devon get out of his mom's car, ignoring her as best he can.

"Hey, Ash," he says. "Hey, Ian."

He steps right in front of Max and cuts him out of our circle without saying hello.

"Hey, Devon," says Max, his face stormy. "Mommy dropped her special boy off today, huh?"

"Did anyone else hear a giant sucking sound?" Devon says.

Max barely has time to get angry before Devon adds, "Oh, hey, Max! You ready to have fun today?"

"It'd be a real shame if we didn't get to have a little *fun*, you and me," says Max.

"Was that a threat?" Devon asks, a little bit confused.

"Are you a moron?"

Everyone freezes.

"What did you say?" says Devon.

Max looks right at Devon and presses on: "Hey, Ian, is Devon a moron?"

"Uh . . ." My face goes blank.

"Leave him out of this." Devon isn't used to someone challenging him at his own game, and he shoves Max with his elbow.

It's a good thing Mark's bus arrives just then. He runs up to us with a big smile. "Field Day! Come on, guys, what're you waiting for?"

I guess no one has a good answer to that, so we hurry inside. Everyone except Max. He just stands there, watching the crowd disappear. The sad music playing inside his skull is so loud I can hear it too.

"Hey," I call back to him. "You coming, Max?"

He gives this look like he can't tell if I'm making fun of him. But before he can say anything, Mark yells, "Ian, come on!" and I chase after my friends.

Screwing Up Field Day

As I plop at my desk, I feel the back of my neck tingle and, looking over my shoulder, catch a glimpse of Amy glaring at me. Trying to set me on fire with her eyes, from the look of things.

"Hey, Amy," I say.

"Yes?" she says coldly.

I don't get it. Is she still mad from yesterday?

I could *ask*, I guess, but then she'd know I'm confused—and if the first rule for being a kid is be quiet and fit in, the second rule is never let on when there's something you don't understand. Just agree with what the other kids are saying, or be really vague, or pull the fire alarm maybe.

Before I can do any of that, the classroom door slams shut and Mr. Dunford calls out, "Good morning, almost middle schoolers! Everyone excited to go outside?"

The room erupts in a cheer.

"Good. We just have one piece of business to get out of the way. Everyone please take out your reflections and pass them forward."

Suddenly the air is full of riffling sounds as everyone passes up their assignments. And I'm trying to think of a way to get Dunford to go easy on me when Amy whacks me in the shoulder with a stack of papers—

I pass them forward without pausing and Amy sighs as she figures out I forgot.

"Don't tell him, Ian," says Mark from the next row over. "He might not notice . . ."

I think about pretending I turned in my reflection, but pretty much right away my whole body goes hot and cold at the same time. Nope. Not an option.

"Mr. Dunford?" I say. "I forgot."

"That's not a problem, Ian," says Dunford. "I'll stay inside with you as long as it takes for you to finish."

"Wow," says Mark, passing my desk on his way outside. "Way to screw up our Field Day, Ian." He shakes his head and abandons me to my fate. At least Ash gives me a little smile as he runs outside to have fun. But then they're all gone and I'm alone in the classroom, feeling lame.

I stare at the blank piece of paper in front of me, trying to focus: How do words work? Was I even *in* this class this year? With every cheer and splash, my eyes go to the windows.

"All right," Dunford says at last. "Are you writing a novel, Ian? Bring me what you have."

As I hand over my five hard-earned sentences, he takes a quick look and holds the paper up, like it's a dead fish I put on his desk. "You missed the point of this exercise, you know."

"I don't know what you want!" I say.

He lifts an eyebrow.

"Mr. Dunford, come on. Please?"

He doesn't move.

"It's the last day, Mr. Dunford. If I don't get it by now . . ."

For a long time he just watches. Waiting. "All right, Ian," he says in a voice he can't make sound stern. "Just copy it down neatly. You can go outside."

By the time I get outside I'm a tornado in the shape of a kid. I run through half the activities with an intensity that's never been seen at East Huron Elementary. At one point I manage to combine beanbag toss and water balloons into a supersport that should probably be in the Olympics.

But before I can perfect it we're called inside for lunch. I'm halfway through explaining the rules when Devon says, "We get it, Ian. Give it a rest!"

And when I look up at him, I realize that I've forgotten the very first rule: keep quiet until you know what other people want to hear.

"Sure, Dev," I say.

"Whatever." His eyes linger on my food. My peanut butter and jelly sandwich, apple, and sensible granola bar. His expression softens a little.

"I'm sorry, dude," he says. "Wanna trade?"

"Really?" I ask. Devon's lunch is a big upgrade: cold pizza and Fritos.

He nods and pushes it across the table. "Not really hungry."

"You sure?" I ask. "Thanks, man."

For the rest of lunch Ash and I recite old jokes and Mark and Devon argue about sports, and then all our heads turn at once as we see the teachers bringing out ice cream and cookies. Which is when a cough escapes the little table where Max is sitting.

Devon and Mark look at each other immediately.

"You okay, Maxy?" Devon calls out.

When I turn, Max is nearly white and his eyes are really wide. He tries to say something, but he can't get a word out. There's just this weird whistling sound . . .

The other kids at the table with Max must know what's going on. "Nurse Mike!" they call out as Max fumbles with a terrifying needle.

Next thing I know, that crazy-looking thing is sticking out of Max's thigh. It all happens so fast I can barely keep up, and even Devon looks scared. Max's lips have turned blue—he's wheezing like he can't breathe and I don't know if it's been a second or a minute or an hour . . . but at the end of it a hand tightens on my upper arm. It's the lunch lady. "Come with me."

"What?" I ask.

"*Now.*"

"But—"

"Not a word."

The voice carries so much weight that I jump to obey, and as I'm led through the hall I see Mark and Devon and Ash there too. They look angry. Or afraid.

An ambulance waits outside the school and a stretcher rolls into the hall. Looking back to the lunchroom I can see Max is on his feet, insisting on walking to the ambulance himself.

He avoids looking at us mostly, but there's one moment when our eyes connect and I almost feel like I can't breathe now, either.

Does he think *we* hurt him?

Devil Sludge

I've never been to the principal's office before. It's a weird combination of library and dungeon and twice as musty smelling as either one. The only sound comes from the wall clock's ticking and the muffled voices in the hall: the gods, discussing our fate.

I jump a little when the door swings open and our principal comes in with an unreadable expression.

"Hello, boys." She looks us all over. "Devon Crawford . . . I know you. Who are your friends?"

Ash and Mark mumble their names, and suddenly my friends seem weirdly unfamiliar to me. Like we're robots playing the role of ourselves. I'm last to say my name, and when I do, she makes me say it three times until it's loud enough to hear.

I've never been treated like this by grown-ups before. Like I've committed some crime, and I have no idea what I did.

"Ms. King?" Devon asks. "What happened to Max?"

The principal takes a long, hard look at Devon before she answers.

"Max has an allergy to peanuts, Devon. That's why we have a special place in the cafeteria for him to eat. Did you know that?"

"*That* was allergies?" Devon asks with surprise.

"Boys, did you know that Max was allergic to peanuts?"

Ash nods. The rest of us look at him.

Ms. King sits down on the edge of her desk. "Okay, I'm still a little confused about what happened. Can someone explain to me what's been going on between you boys and Max Willis, please?"

She pauses, but no one volunteers. I can feel her eyes linger on me, even though I'm looking at my shoes and thinking back to trading my sandwich.

"Ian?" she says. "Help me understand."

I feel my heart trying to escape from my rib cage, and all of my words stick in my throat. Just like usual. I don't know what to say, and I can't look at my friends . . . but all of them are being quiet, so it feels like that's what I should be doing too. It's my only choice, I guess, since I've lost the power of speech.

The principal looks disappointed. She turns back to Devon and says, "Okay. Well you're free to go for now, boys."

A wave of relief washes over me.

"We are?" Ash says, surprised.

"Yes."

"Really?" says Mark.

"Ash, Mark? Your parents are here to take you home. I'll let them talk to you about what's going to happen next. Devon, Ian? Your parents couldn't make it, so you've got detention with Mr. Dunford for the afternoon. We'll pick this up next week."

Something about the shock of the words *next week* unfreezes my tongue again. "Next week is vacation, Ms. King," I remind her. "Today's the last day of school."

Principal King's face forms a smile, but there's absolutely no amusement in her expression. "Mr. Hart," she says, "you don't think that you boys are still getting a summer vacation after what happened today, do you?"

"Because of my sandwich?" I squeak.

"If you want to act like bullies, then that's how you'll be treated," she says. And then she keeps going, but I can't really understand it very well—

There's this dull ringing in my ears, and her voice sounds like it's very far away, even though she's right there in front of me. I feel this weird separation between my mind and my body, and all I can figure out is that she's sending us to a summer school or something—a reform school full of bullies.

Bullies like *me*.

As I try to wrap my head around everything that's going on, the world moves forward without me. We leave the principal's office, and Devon and I go to Mr. Dunford's room. He's sitting at a little desk in the back, like a student does.

You might expect we'd be copying lines from the board or something—but Mr. Dunford "just wants to talk."

And I *want* to talk—I want to confess. To apologize. To stop everything, and go back.

"Mr. Dunford?" I begin. But then I stop. I can't find any words that will send me back in time and fix everything. And also Devon glares at me with such ferocity that I decide to keep my mouth shut very, very tight.

"What's up, Ian?" says Mr. Dunford with lifted eyebrows.

I can feel Devon's eyes drilling into my skull.

". . . . can I go to the bathroom, please?"

When you need to be alone, there's no place like a huge, empty bathroom with a tiny, lockable stall. Other people might listen to their favorite song, or have a snack, or pick on a kid who can't fight back, but when I need a break from it all, I come here. You can escape for three and a half minutes—be alone without worrying what other people think.

I close the lid on the toilet and sit down on top with my knees to my chest.

It was my *sandwich* that did all this. The thought of that tiny peanut rips me free of earth's gravity and sends me drifting in the darkness—like I'm in outer space, silent and frozen and alone.

My brain replays the morning over and over, and with every replay I feel my heart sucked down all over again. Like it's being flushed down the toilet, pulling the rest of me with it into some other place and some alternate when.

And then that story I heard in class yesterday bubbles up in my mind.

Thomas Edison, what would you do if you were here?

You didn't start out a famous scientist. You were my age once—how did you survive it all? How did you transform from a twelve-year-old dropout to a self-taught inventor guy?

I wait for an answer from young Thomas Edison, but he stays very quiet.

Like he's not even there.

And I pull my heart back out of the toilet and push the lever to flush. I want to go back to my real life, but everything feels different as I try to stand up.

The sound of that flush, like an angry wolverine gargling, makes my head swirl with it . . . like I'm spinning and spinning, out of control. Into some awful and blurry new future.

The Juvenile Academy for Noncompliant and Underachieving Students

It feels like the car is going off the edge of a cliff, but every time I look out the window the road is solid beneath us.

"We'll be at the school soon, honey," says Mom. Reform school, she means. I'm going to a new school, full of bullies. I stare out the window, trying to match up my old life with this new one. The last few days have been such a weird, fuzzy forever. I haven't heard from Devon or Mark, or even Ash. I haven't *wanted* to talk to them, really, but still it'd be nice to be reminded I'm not alone.

All I've wanted this week is sleep—but sleep is impossible for me now, so I've played a lot of video games. When I play video games I can almost forget what happened to Max. But after a while I'll be sitting there and there'll be this explosion. Except it's not the stuff on the screen, it's the guilt in my chest.

Your friend Max could've died, I hear in my head.

And there I am, video game music playing and an impossible world whooshing past on the TV—it's all turned into dumb little dots. My eyes go unfocused and objects scroll past, and I push the controls to the right so my character gets knocked off a cliff and tumbles off the edge of the world.

It feels good to destroy your hard work sometimes.

But only for a minute. Because then you have to beat the whole level again—setting the table, pushing food around your plate, taking out the trash. Only, halfway through you stop and realize it's not a video game.

It's your stupid life.

And then you find yourself sitting in your room with your huge duffel bag packed for this crazy summer school thing, and that little freak in your head reminds you about the thousand-page list of banned items that came in your admission packet. So you dump everything out again and repack a toothbrush and some underwear and sit there with that sad little bundle, and start to laugh.

The Freak in my head likes to laugh when there's nothing funny about what's going on. It likes to speak up when I should probably stay quiet. It wants to consume me and take control for good—and it's always there, lurking and waiting for its moment . . .

And right now, driving to reform school, I feel the Freak's laughter roll around inside me like a silent scream, drowning out all of Mom's "we love yous" and "we'll miss yous" and "don't panics"—which is probably not a bad thing, because saying "don't panic" only makes me panic more.

Is this stupid thing ever going to plummet off a cliff or what?

But the car just rumbles onto the highway exit ramp, like a turtle slides into a river. We turn onto a gravel road, bumper to bumper with other cars ferrying doomed children to the Juvenile Academy for Noncompliant and Underachieving Students. JANUS.

"There it is!" says Dad, pointing at a building that must be the school. "Looks okay, right?"

"It's so pretty!" says Mom.

It does look pretty from a distance, I guess. It's this sprawling, green campus, and the buildings have these huge, bright banners hung all around. There's hardly any hint of the grimness that lurks in the hearts of the bullies who will come to call this place home.

That's the way it usually is with evil, though. First it lurks—then it leaps up and clobbers you, like a big cat in the jungle.

And that's what this place is, right? A jungle. With fields full of poisonous flowers and endless stretches of quicksand bog. And this one crazy valley where the angry monkeys live. You know, the angry monkeys in those gnarled, ancient trees with fruit shaped like dodgeballs? Oh! You don't know about the dodgeball monkeys? If you're gonna die, dodgeball monkeys are a decent choice. Top five maybe. Solid top ten for sure. I can almost hear the sounds of their bruising artillery across the open fields when Dad shuts the engine off.

"You ready, kid?" he says.

Okay, Hart, I tell myself. *One thing at a time. Breathe, then once you've got the breathing thing down you can try opening the car door. Now. Pick up your bag and don't look around.*

My heart is beating a little too hard and I take a second to control my breathing.

Just put one foot in front of the other. Good man. Now keep walking, but listen to me: hugging Mom and Dad good-bye's gonna be hard, so let's not get caught by surprise, okay? Start working up to that now while you're walking to that check-in table. Go.

I take one last step, and there I am. The pink bunting around the table does a rumba in the breeze.

"Hart," I say. "Ian Ontario."

Something just tells me to do it last name, first name like that. The clerk gives me a bored smile, and I sign this really long document right on the dotted line.

"Yersinia Pestis." I hear a girl behind me announce herself. It's almost like she's challenging the clerk to disagree with her.

"Pestis, Pestis—don't see that last name here," says the clerk.

"That's because it's the scientific name for bubonic plague," says someone else. I look and see it's a teacher with a shaved head and leather jacket, a lopsided smile on his face. "What's your real name, young lady?"

"Alva," she says begrudgingly.

"Last name?" he presses.

The girl puffs up with pride. She covers her mouth and whispers, so no one but the teacher can hear—but by the way he reacts, it's pretty clear the girl has a reason for giving a fake name. Probably because her real one is the sort of thing that would make life much harder in bully school.

"Well, you can't be Yersinia," the teacher says after a minute. He turns to the clerk. "Write down Alva Anonymous, Matty."

The girl considers this, and gives an approving nod.

Past the table I start toward the innocent-looking building that is to be my new home for the next six weeks. But I've hardly taken ten steps when I a big hand lifts my bag off my shoulder—

"Students over there, kid," says that teacher with the shaved head. On a scale from one to Evil Mastermind, he's somewhere around Henchman from the look of him. The sort of guy who does the villain's dirty work. And he's staring at me like I'm a human pile of underwear.

"The bus," says the henchman, heaving my bag onto a heap of luggage. "You know what a bus is?"

I'm just standing and staring like a moron. My whole "one thing at a time" strategy is crumbling around me.

A smile creeps across my face and I nod. "The bus?" I say, pointing at it like a baby does.

Crap. What am I *doing* right now? This is all a horrible mistake. I need to turn around.

"Okay, Ian!" says Dad. "We've gotta say bye now."

I make a sound that fails to turn into words. It's the groan of a dinosaur being crushed into oil over millions and millions of years.

"You gonna be all right, buddy?" says Mom.

I manage to smile so she doesn't worry. "Sure. I'm good."

"Okay, Ian." Mom tells me everything she said in the car all over again, and as much as I try to hold on to her words, they go right through me. Everything except the last thing: ". . . and don't let Devon boss you around, all right?"

I nod at her, but I know that's a promise I'm gonna break.

They're both looking at me with such big, nervous smiles that I'm tearing up before I know it.

This is not the way to survive bully school, Hart! says that voice in the back of my head.

And I turn to the bus, which looks new and shiny—the biggest lie in the universe. There might be a coat of paint on that machine, but underneath it's rotted through. The rusted engine that pulls it is full of screaming, tortured gears. And I have no idea where it's heading, or what I'm supposed to do once I'm there.

So I just climb on and press Restart, and the next level of this crazy game comes to life all around me.

Bullies Like Me

When I step on the bus, a lightbulb appears in my head. A soft glow leaks from my ears, and it's probably a lot like how it feels to have a crazy idea for an invention that will change the world—but in this case, the world is not changing for the better. This lightbulb in my head is a warning: Something is very wrong with this scene.

What's wrong, you ask? Good question, imaginary Thomas Edison! I like when you don't completely ignore me.

The answer is: It's too calm. *Way* too calm—and if you hadn't dropped out of school you'd know exactly how dangerous it is when all the other kids get quiet. There are things you learn in class that aren't math and US history, you know. Wisdom passed down from those who came before us . . . those ancients who grow hair in weird places and get super moody for no apparent reason.

One of the most important new-kid rules? If there are bullies around—and there are almost always bullies around—the first thing to do is identify their Target. Because if you can't figure out who the Target is, you can be pretty sure they're looking for one.

And I promise, Tom: You do not want it to be you.

That's why I really have to find a seat on this bus right now. But I'd like to keep talking to you, inside my head, if that's okay? I hope it's okay. It sorta helps me not get so nervous, having someone to distract me while I'm going down the aisle here.

As I put one foot in front of the other, I see a girl scoop up a little puff of orange fuzz and stuff it into the pocket of her sweatshirt—it's a tiny guinea pig, and I smile in the girl's direction. But she doesn't look back. Just when I'm about to ask to sit by her anyway, this other, cooler girl plops down into the seat. Crap.

I continue down the aisle under the watchful gaze of a bunch of scary-looking kids. Any second they could fix on me as their Target, but I make it past and find a couple empty rows in the middle of the bus.

I'm right across the aisle from a boy in bifocals now. Score. With his old-man glasses, this kid's sure to become the Target. But after I get a closer look at him, I realize I'm completely wrong.

This is no victim. This is a boy who has *hardened* under the taunting. Who has learned that the best defense is to strike first. His eyes are dead now. Fiery, cruel mirrors. Cross him at your own risk. I don't want to sit anywhere *near* this kid—but it's too late to change course: He's already watching me.

So I slide into the window seat across from Deadeyes.

And outside I see my parents' car. Mom and Dad are standing next to it, like they're gonna wait here until this bus leaves their sight.

Last chance to make a run for it, Hart, the Freak tells me.

I feel a hollow thing in my chest as I think about all the stuff I'm gonna miss out on this summer: My dog. My room. The way things were a week ago, when I was so excited to be finished with elementary school. When my friends and I were dizzy with summer dreams, and the possibilities went on forever—

Before the peanut butter and jelly jam.

How could I have been so gullible, Tom? Did I know on some level the *real* reason Devon wanted to trade lunches with me? Was I so much of a pushover that I would look the other way and let something terrible happen to Max?

Did I want so badly to belong?

Well, now I do belong. Right here with the rest of these jerks.

Listen, Tom: Forget about that stuff I was saying before, all right? You should just go away while you can.

If I want to survive this, I need to stop having imaginary ghost friends and conversations with myself all the time. I need to keep my head down and be normal. Fade into the background, like a chameleon.

And in the likely event that I *don't* survive? If that happens, we can *totally* be ghost friends and haunt cool stuff together. I promise I'll tell you the whole story of how I died in reform school. And it'll be funny. We can haunt my killer!

"Ian Hart!" A familiar voice startles me from my thoughts and I look up at Devon's smiling face bobbing toward me. "Long time no see."

He gives me a high five and thuds down into the seat next to me. "Whatcha been up to?"

My mind races for something to tell him.

"Stuff. Video games." I don't tell him anything specific about the levels I can't seem to beat—and luckily, Mark and Ash are right behind him to distract us from these questions. Everyone plops down around me.

"Hey, Ian!" says Ash as he cranes over the seat in front of me, looking really excited. Excited to see me, I realize, with a little burst of happiness. "Have you been saving the good riddles?"

"Ohh . . . I completely forgot to bring them."

"*Seriously?*" he moans. He makes this exaggerated show of throwing up his hands. "Well at least I brought you something to read."

He opens his hoodie and pulls out a slim book.

"Oooh," I say. "What *is* it?"

"This," says Ash, "is a book called *The Hitchhiker's Guide to the Galaxy*. You need to know about it. It tells you how to survive if the planet blows up, and it's also funny."

"Where'd you get this? In that spooky used bookstore we found?"

"Nope! It's my *dad's*!" says Ash. "He says it's way too advanced for me, but I think he may have been trying to reverse-psychology me."

"And it worked, didn't it?" I say with a raised eyebrow.

"Who cares? It's probably the best thing ever!" says Ash. "Wait until you read it."

With an enormous grin, I try to take it from him, but Ash pulls it back and gives me a warning. "It's my dad's favorite book, but he told me I could keep it with me this summer as long as I took special care of it. Guard it with your life."

"Promise," I say.

"No bending the spine like you always do."

I glare at him. "You have any other rules?"

"Only one. You gotta finish it fast. I need to talk about it with someone."

"Yes, sir."

"I've already been waiting all week, 'cause you weren't around. Where'd you disappear to?"

One of the best things about Ash Franklin is that Ash

Franklin talks to me like the voices in my head don't. He's clear and straightforward and he never loses focus, and I would not be shocked at all to learn that Ash is some sort of superhero in disguise, and that I'm his sidekick, and the whole audience feels bad for me because of how sad it is that I hang around with a superhero all the time and I never even know it.

Just then the back of the bus erupts in *ooh*s. That girl who gave a fake name at the registration table glares daggers at this human beanstalk with a straggly mustache under his nose. I can tell she's about to punch him—but then she thinks again.

She mutters something that makes him blink in confusion.

I watch like I'm hypnotized as the girl covers her head with her hoodie and stomps up the aisle toward the front of the bus. And the boy looks after her, like he kinda wants her to come back—but when she doesn't turn around, he just sinks into his seat again in silence.

"What're you staring at, kid?" the girl barks at me.

"I'm not staring . . ."

I *want* to turn away but it's like those eyes of hers are magnets. Or lasers, burning a hole straight through me. There's definitely something weird going on. Maybe this girl was recruited to be an international spy in the third grade, and had secret lasers implanted in her retinas or something?

Then I realize what's off: This girl is *a lot* older than me.

I turn to Ash. "Is that girl—?"

"Like fourteen?" says Ash.

"Yeah."

"It's not just her, either," he whispers. "Everyone on this bus is older than we are . . ."

He gestures around in a secretive way. And I follow with my eyes, trying to be sneaky about it. He's right: We're the youngest kids on the bus.

"Actually," says Mark quietly, "we're the youngest kids in the whole school."

We both turn to Mark slowly.

"You guys didn't know?" he adds. "There aren't any elementary school kids allowed in this place."

"You mean except for us?" I say.

"We're not in elementary school anymore, Ian," says Ash.

"Nope," says Mark. "We're middle schoolers now."

Sink or Swim

"**W**elcome to orientation, swimming salmon!" A booming voice comes over the bus's overhead speakers.

I blink. "Did he just call us—?"

"Yes! Swimming salmon is what we call our students here," the voice says. "You'll see why soon enough. For now, let me say how glad I am to see you were all able to join us this morning."

Ash turns to face me. "Probably because if we didn't show up he'd've sent the FBI to hunt us down."

"My name is Judge Cressett"—the voice goes on—"and I am the head of this academy. But you may call me 'Your Honor' if you prefer."

Ash and I swap grins at this.

"If you have any concerns, you can rest assured that I, your teachers, and KinderCorp all take them very seriously. It's sink or swim here at JANUS, and we all want you to swim. It's in a fish's nature to swim, after all . . . for a salmon to follow its instincts, and swim upstream—"

"And get eaten by a bear?" I whisper to Ash.

"—returning home with a new appreciation for—"

"The digestive tract of the common brown bear," Ash whispers back.

The disembodied voice makes a throat-clearing sound. "Boys, is there a problem?"

Ash and I stop and look around for the Judge, but we can't see him anywhere.

"Can he see us?" I ask Mark.

"And *hear* you!" the Judge's voice declares. "Now. I'm trying to give you some important information about our academy. You don't want to start off on the wrong foot in this discipline— do you?"

"No, Your Honor," says Mark.

"Good," says the Judge. "Then shut up and listen. This is all very important. The Juvenile Academy for Noncompliant and Underachieving Students, which we call JANUS, is named for a god from Roman antiquity with one face on the front of his head and another face on the back of it."

And I immediately blackout from boredom, but even in my unconscious state, the voice somehow drills into my skull:

"Janus was known as the master of beginnings and endings; he looked to the future and kept an eye on the past—and here at JANUS these things are rather important to us as well."

It's like he's speaking another language, Tom. Or . . . have I forgotten how to speak English? Do the teachers at bully school have special powers to make us forget stuff? Control our *minds*?

The torture goes on:

"—your goals in perspective, you will be successful at this academy, but if you do not succeed in this discipline," he says, "you will not go back home at the end of the summer. Your next stop will be the KinderCorp's Children's Village."

I hear Ash make a weird noise.

"What's wrong?" I mumble, looking over the seat in front of me.

"The Village," he says. "It gives me the creeps."

"Yeah," I say. Then, after a second, "Wait, why?"

"The Children's Village?" he whispers. "Are you messing around?"

"No messing around," I say. "What is it?"

Ash frowns and pulls on his sleeves like he does when he's really uncomfortable. "You don't know about the Village?"

"You *really* don't know?" Mark says, craning back around to me. "Did you read the letter you just signed at registration?"

"The letter?"

"Your *confession*, Ian," says Mark.

"My *what*?"

"Boys!" says the Judge over the loudspeaker. "I am still talking. Do I need to tell you again what will happen if you fail in this discipline?"

"No, sir," says Mark. "If we fail, then you will take the confession that we just signed, and you'll use it to send us away to juvenile detention." Mark looks right at me and Ash when he says this. "The Children's Village," he whispers, at the same time I figure it out myself.

And I feel the moment stretch out, more and more. And the space between my next two heartbeats lasts seventy-five years. I get older and older, and my hair and my fingernails get longer and longer, and eventually I'm on my deathbed surrounded by friends and family and robots. Mostly robots. And then I'm reborn and I repeat all the exact same mistakes, only this time everybody makes their own food out of sunlight like plants do. It's kinda cool, actually, except for the whole thing where I end up right back where I started again: in reform school, on this bus, facing the fact that I've confessed to a bully crime and didn't even know it.

"Look, it's one of those things that sounds way worse than it is," says Ash as the bus jolts to the left.

"Totally," Mark agrees. "As long as we don't fail here it'll all get wiped away . . ."

"It will?" I ask.

"Yep, that's the deal," says Mark.

"But if we *do* fail," says Devon with a terrible smile, "we get sent to you-know-where."

KinderCorp. A state-of-the-art behavioral modification

facility and artisanal punishment institute. With a built-in coal mine, and eleven levels of parking.

As I come to understand just how big my problems are, I suddenly feel like the bus is crumpling around me like a tin can. I need to get off this thing and go somewhere I can be alone for five minutes. Somewhere I don't have to smile and pretend I'm not scared. I need a bathroom break, Tom.

And so it's an enormous relief when the bus groans to a halt. I push off in front of everyone else—but when I get outside, I freeze in place . . .

We're in the middle of the woods.

Stranded with a Stachesquatch

"**W**hat're we doing in the middle of the woods?" I ask.

As if in response, the door slams shut and the bus roars as it starts to move back down the road.

"We're being stranded," says the boy with the horrible dead eyes.

"Why are we *being stranded* in the middle of the woods?" I ask him.

"They're testing us, I think," says Mark. "See what we do when we crack."

"Some of us are already pre-cracked," says Deadeyes, looking right at me.

Devon rolls his eyes and grabs the collar of my shirt. "Sink or swim, Ian."

Mark and Devon and Ash and I stick together as we follow the rest of the bullies into the wilderness. Out of the corner of my eye, I see a baby monkey following that beanstalk kid from the bus. It might have been my imagination, but it doesn't really matter, because as soon as I start thinking about hearing a distant *sproinngg!* of a dodgeball, I burst out laughing. That's the Freak coming through, Tom. It plays tricks when things get intense. Makes me laugh, even when nothing about the situation is funny. *Keep it together*, I tell myself. I could *really* use a couple minutes alone in a bathroom.

"Are we almost there?" Ash asks hopefully.

"Nope!" says this woman with dark, shimmery blue hair and tattoos of feathers going up her arm.

"So when we get back, what happens next?" I follow up, keeping my eyes peeled for any monkeys.

"Don't be so eager, boys," says the blue-haired woman. "Just enjoy the sunshine and let it all happen in due course."

"What if I don't like surprises?" Devon asks.

"Or sunlight?" says the girl named Alva. I have no idea how long she has been there, due to monkey watch.

I can see the woman smirk. "You need to let *go* a little, kids. If you're always in a rush to get somewhere else, when will you get where you're going?"

Mark frowns. "Never?"

"Correct!"

"So . . . how exactly are you *supposed* to get where you want to go?" says Ash.

She shrugs. "Just stop and look around: You're already there."

Ash stops. He looks around.

"I am not where I want to be," he says.

Before I know what's happening, I feel another bubble of laughter erupt like a volcano—and I shut it down as fast as I can, but not before I've attracted attention.

"Something funny about being stranded in the woods?" says a boy with hair like a spiky helmet and a hypnotizing movie-star stare.

His aggressive, bright-white Cheshire cat smile makes me jump back—directly into the giant beanstalk with the mustache.

"Watch where you're walking."

The beanstalk pushes me forward into this giant puddle that wraps around my wrists and drains down around my foot inside my shoe.

I look up, and Mark is standing over me. "You okay?"

I can hear that guy with the mustache cackling and I see Devon fighting off a grin.

"What happened here?" The teacher with the shaved head who looks like a supervillain's sidekick catches up with us.

"Nothing," says Mark. "My friend just slipped."

"Well get him up. Don't fall behind."

As the man clomps away, the mustached beanstalk keeps laughing at me.

"Back off, Sasquatch," says Devon.

"What'd you call me?" asks the boy, standing up to his full height—about a head taller than any of us.

"You heard me," says Devon. "Walk away before I punch those diseased follicles right off your lip."

There's a laugh from behind me—an audience is gathering, sniffing for a fight.

"Dev, come on," says Mark. "Let's go."

This makes the beanstalk smile. "Good advice. You better listen to your mother."

Devon grins. "Way better advice than whoever told you to grow that caterpillar on your face, Sasquatch. *Stache*squatch."

"Funny thing coming from a ten-year-old," says the Stachesquatch.

Devon's eyes gleam with devilish delight. "At least I'm human," he says. "Not some woodland creature who lost all its fur from overconsumption of Mountain Dew."

The Stachesquatch goes cold.

And Devon looks down at me. "Ian. What're you still doing on the ground, man?"

I really have no answer to that.

"Come on, Ian," I hear Mark whisper to me. "Stand up, okay?"

"Yeah, Ian," says the Stache. "Stand up, Ian. Let's get on with this, *Ian* . . ."

"Don't be an idiot," Mark tells him. "If we start a fight out here, we'll all get sent to the Village before reform school even *starts*."

The Stache hesitates for just a second, and Mark keeps at him. "Good decision," he says, pulling me to my feet.

"Ever seen a bear that went bald, guys?" Devon calls out to everyone. "It's just *sad*."

This is how Mark and Devon are when their friends are in trouble, Tom. Devon's the brawn, and Mark's the brains. Except that Devon's also the brains. And Mark's no wimp.

The Stache watches the four of us continue on, sort of perplexed at how we escaped him, and frowns. "I'll see you later," he says in a way that makes me feel queasy. "That's a promise from Cole Harper."

"What's that, pal?" Devon shouts back. "Didn't hear ya."

"I said, it's a promise from Cole Harper."

"Sorry, didn't catch it."

"Ask Ian," says Cole Harper. "He gets it, doesn't he?"

And even though I feel shivers down my back, Ash keeps me marching forward, away from Cole "the Stachesquatch" Harper, until he's out of earshot.

"Our boy's a great negotiator, right?" says Devon, grabbing Mark around the neck as we head down the trail.

Mark's a pretty good talker, I guess you'd say. The whole Wheeler family is made up of lawyers and school board members and a mayor or two.

"It wasn't hard," says Mark. "It's just a matter of mutually assured destruction."

"Mutually assured destruction?" I ask.

"It means that if we fight, nobody wins. Everyone gets sent

to the Village—so we have to find a way to live together, even if we're not happy about it."

"You explained that to him?" I ask, looking back in the Stache's direction.

Mark nods.

"In small words so he could understand?" Ash adds.

"Guys, let it go!"

We let it go. But I'm still worried, Tom: As everyone knows, there are plenty of ways to tease, taunt, and torture someone that don't leave a physical mark.

The Last Stall on the Right

"**W**here'd you go, Hart?" says Devon as I slide down the table next to my friends at the dining hall that night. I was trying to disappear and get two minutes alone, but I don't tell anyone that. Can't show any weakness, Tom.

But we haven't gotten a break yet. Not after surviving that hike—or those weird trust exercises the teachers made us do to "learn about each other." My stomach is a tight ball and my mouth is so dry I can't swallow right. But now dinner's here. That's something, right?

Ash pushes a little plate into the middle of the table for me. "Pie was going fast," he says. "Got you some lemon meringue, though."

"It's so fluffy." I drag the pie with its creamy, foamy peaks toward me. "You're the best, Ash."

He shrugs. "One of the many services I provide."

Before I can even settle into enjoying my pie, I feel the *slam* of a dinner tray against the table. The force of the crash sends earthquakes through my more gelatinous food items, and from behind me comes a horrible voice.

"Anyone sitting here?" says the Stache. I mean, Cole. "Pretty crazy first day, huh?" he adds, squeezing his giant body onto the bench. Cole doesn't wait for an answer. He just smirks and snarfs about half of my lemon meringue pie in one bite.

"Mmm, good pie!" he manages to get out, along with a spray of food particles. His version of "sharing," I guess. Then there's that wide, grinning mouth . . . daring us to say anything.

"It's always a big decision, right?" Devon breaks the silence.

"What's that?" says Cole.

"Where to sit in the cafeteria of a new school," says Devon.

"Sure is," says Cole with a grin.

As the silence closes in on us again, Alva comes up to us with her tray.

"Mind if I join?" She eyes us all warily and slides down the bench.

Cole sort of smiles at her, and he bumps me down so there's bench next to him. "Make space, dude."

Without looking up, she opens her mouth and says, "You guys are from the same school or something?"

"The four of us," says Ash, pointing at Mark and Devon too. "East Huron Elem—Middle School."

"You can call us the Huron Spawn," I say.

She smirks. "Did you just give yourself your own nickname?"

Cole laughs and I can already feel my cheeks reddening, so I just focus on what I should have been doing the whole time: staying quiet. I watch this Alva Anonymous girl, and the longer she sits with us, the more it feels like maybe she's just jealous we're here with friends. Which I can totally understand, you know?

Ash sees me watching her and looks at me with raised eyebrows, but just then Mark elbows me.

"Ian, come on," he says. "We're leaving now."

I look up and see my friends gathering their things to go.

"Okay, coming."

But when I stand up, something feels wrong. I look down to figure out why but I'm already falling forward—and as I stretch out my arms to break my fall, all the slimy remains of my dinner end up on my clothes and face and down my shirt. I feel it all happening in slow motion, but I don't realize until I'm on the ground looking at my feet:

My shoelaces are tied together.

Cole Harper bursts out laughing, and a bunch of other kids join in too.

And for a second, I see myself like I'm one of them, watching it all happen. My hands, my clothes, everything covered with slime. I'm outside of my own body, looking down on it all.

And the next thing I know, there's a weird *whooshing* sound all around me—like a toilet flushing—and the dining hall starts to stretch out like gum when you're peeling it off the bottom of your shoe. Like the whole world is inside a toilet bowl that someone just flushed.

Great.

Here we go again.

F
L
U
S
H
!

Have you ever been sucked into a black hole, Tom? No? Well, they say your whole body gets stretched out toward infinity by its gravity, and then your whole body gets crushed down to a speck.

Or maybe it's the other way around. Whatever, that's not important. Point is . . . one second ago I was on the ground in a puddle of slime. Then the dining hall got sucked down a drain, and when the world started to make sense again, I was somewhere else.

The boys' bathroom, alone in a locked stall.

This used to happen to me a lot when I was younger. I'd

give the wrong answer in front of the whole class, or take a kickball to the stomach and fall down, and my head would get really hot and everything would go blurry, like I was about to pass out . . . and the next thing I knew, I'd be in the boys' bathroom all by myself, with no memory of how I got there.

I'd just be sitting on top of the toilet, head between my knees. And I could *feel* the toilet flushing, in the very center of my being. Like, I know that's weird—but it's true. I could feel my heart swirling around some cosmic vortex. As if it had gotten sucked right out of my chest and into the porcelain U-bend.

And in my head, the embarrassing thing I did just kept playing on loop. Over and over. The cosmo-flush happened again and again, and there I was: back at the beginning of the nightmare once more.

Time travel isn't like it is in the movies, Tom. It really sucks.

But eventually the swirling vortex has always slowed down and stopped. And I remind myself it'll happen again today.

After a million slow-motion replays of the dining hall, the toilet will stop being a time machine and become a toilet again. And the bathroom will just be a bathroom.

And so when it does I do what I have to do: I pull my heart up from the pipes by the arteries—very, very carefully—and Scotch tape it back into place, and I walk out, back to my prison cell full of bullies. Just in time for lights-out.

Our dorm has about a dozen bunk beds, including one that's got my name on the card at the end. I climb up into it, shucking off my shoes and socks as I go, fumbling my way through the dark.

Devon's already asleep as I climb above him into my bunk. He doesn't even twitch, just keeps sleeping soundly, no matter what's in his way. Why can't I be like that?

I freeze in place. There's a hulking shadow in my bed—

"Ian? Get up here!"

"Ash! You freaked me out."

"I think we should keep watch tonight," he says.

"I don't have a watch," I tell him.

"Ian. I meant that we should stay up and make sure no one tries anything funny while the other guys sleep."

"Oh," I say. "Smart plan. I'll take the first watch."

"Be strong," he says and hands me an invisible watch, which I invisibly fasten around my wrist.

Just then a hand shoots up and grabs his ankle from below.

"Don't slip, Ash," hisses Cole, walking past like nothing happened.

Ash puffs up his chest a little, showing no fear: Ash knows to never let a bully see that they're getting to you.

"You have to sleep *sometime*," whispers the Stache.

"So do you," says Ash.

"And there are two of us, and only one of you," I add.

"Is there only one of me?" says Cole. "Seems like a bit of a, what do you call it . . . an *assumption*."

"Would you all shut *up*?" that kid with perfect hair and teeth barks at us.

Cole turns on him. "*You* shut up!" he yells.

Then there's a shoe flying through the air. It misses me and hits Devon right in the stomach. "Ow!" he grumbles, startling awake. "Who did that?"

The door swings open and the bright hall light spills in.

"Boys!" An angry silhouette stands in the doorway. "You may not talk or be out of your own bed after lights-out."

I try to peer closer. There's something about the voice that's slightly familiar to me. But just as I blink, trying to see who it is, the lights go out again as the door closes with a loud *ka-chunk!*

The Weird Liar Girl Theory

When the sky lightens to an eerie gray, the level starts all over again. I'm back at the very beginning, Tom. Trying to get it right.

It's a gut-punch sort of feeling, starting over, and it knocks my heart loose from the tape that's holding it in place. I feel it smash into the floor with a *thwack!* and when I get my bearings I realize there's a blaring alarm playing through all the speakers in the school. At first I'm pretty sure there's a fire emergency in the building, but then I realize it's even worse: It's our wake-up call.

"Why is this happening to me?" I moan at the uncaring universe.

By the time my brain catches up with my body, I've got my school uniform jacket halfway buttoned up—the only problem is that I've got my legs through the armholes. It does not work very well as pants.

"My jacket smells like old people and gym class," says Devon, pouring himself into his uniform.

"Two great smells, together at last," says Mark.

"Matches with the weird color, though," I mumble.

"I kinda think it works on me, guys," says Ash, and when I look up he's climbing out of his bunk in his puke-colored clothing.

Hold on, I didn't tell you about the uniform yet? Whoa. Well! It's like the sort of jacket and pants that people wear to a funeral—except it's this weird, pukey sort of color.

Pink, Tom. Only, it's not pink, they told us. It's *salmon. Since when is salmon a color,* you may be asking yourself. Turns out it totally *is* a color. It's midway between coral and puce . . . which are also colors. The world is a strange place.

"So, Ian," says Ash in the dining hall at breakfast. "How does it feel being the youngest kid in a school bursting with juvenile delinquents?"

He holds an invisible microphone in front of my mouth, and even though I'm so tired that the air feels like it's as thick as soup, and twice as hard to breathe, I smile like I've just won a big contest and I'm starting my acceptance speech:

"Wow, such an honor, Ash. I never imagined I'd know what it feels like to be this lucky . . ."

"*So* lucky," Ash agrees. "What're you looking forward to the most this summer?"

"Oh man. There's so much. I can't really choose, but for sure I can't wait to be pummeled by everyone in this whole entire place."

"We're all looking forward to that, I think," says Ash into the mic. "What else do you want to say to the viewers at home?"

I shove him and grab the fake microphone: "I'd like to dedicate this to Louie the Grade-Five Hamster," I say. "Louie, you peed on us every day and I will never, ever forget you."

"Or your many fluids," Ash agrees.

That's when I notice a little snort from a couple tables away.

Alva Anonymous. She doesn't look back at us or anything, but she knows we're listening . . .

"You know," she says, "in my school, class pets weren't allowed . . ."

"That sucks," says Ash. "Why not?"

Instead of just answering, she lifts her tray and puts it down next to Ash so she can speak really quietly: "It's probably because of all the mysterious 'accidents' that kept happening."

"Accidents?" I say.

"At night, when no one was around," she adds with a spooky look. "Some kids thought there was a ghost haunting one of the seventh grade lockers, and they said that if it kept happening Principal Nolen was going to have to condemn the whole building . . ."

"Seriously?" I say.

"Yeah." Now she's just getting warmed up. "Nobody knows if it's a ghost or a demon or—"

"—or if it's a weird liar girl with issues?" Devon butts in from across the table.

"It's a theory," she agrees. "The way I've heard the Weird Liar Girl Theory, she has been known to defenestrate people who offend her without the slightest warning. You should watch out for her."

"Defenestrate?" says Ash.

"Chuck 'em out of windows," says Mark.

Alva smiles.

Devon takes a long look at her. "You are so damaged."

But before she can say anything, a tall girl who's probably some sort of cheerleader in her real life walks by with three other girls.

"Nice threads, gentlemen," she says. I summon up enough bravery to smile in her general direction, but then I see she didn't mean this to be a compliment.

"Hello, *Miranda*," says Alva.

Miranda and the other girls are clones now that they're head to toe in pink. Miranda's the head clone, though. That much is clear. And she's got her pant legs rolled up in a certain way and her sleeves cuffed cleverly, and on anyone else it'd look goofy, but on Miranda it looks cool.

As they come closer, I can see a tiny fuzzy head poke out of a jacket pocket . . . and I realize that one of Miranda's clones is that girl from the bus with the guinea pig. I watch the fuzzball grab a giant grape from its owner's hand and snake it into the pocket again, and I smile at the girl.

This time she scowls back at me.

"For your information," says the girl, "if your class hamster peed on you every day, he was probably scared to death of you. Did you ever even think about how he must've felt?"

She turns her back on us and I burn with embarrassment as I wonder if she's right. Louie didn't hate us, did he?

Alva sees my reaction and gives me a little shrug. "Don't let her get to you, Ian. Carrie's great with animals but she assumes that anything that walks on two legs is a total monster."

"Thanks," I say.

"I mean, she's probably right," says Alva, "but don't worry about her right now. Keep your eyes on the cheerleader. Miranda is the most dangerous kid in this whole place."

"Is she?" Devon asks with interest as he flicks his eyes toward Miranda's little gang of mean girls.

Alva glowers darkly at Devon. "*That* girl is evil and she's building an army of conquest. Whatever you're thinking, don't."

"An army?" says Devon, very interested now. "Like, to take over the school or something?"

"Mean-girl problems, huh?" Ash comforts Alva.

Devon snorts. "If we're talking about guys and girls? Let's talk about how unfair these stupid pink uniforms are . . ."

"Meaning what exactly?" says Ash, preening in his jacket.

Devon rolls his eyes. "You know what I mean. It's not fair making dudes wear pink."

"But pink's totally okay for me because I'm a girl?" Alva demands. "Does it *look* like I'm any happier than you are about this situation?"

He stares blankly. "I really can't tell, Alva. Are you?"

"Ugh, never mind."

"What's even grosser?" I say. "Have you seen all the weird graffiti scrawled inside?"

Messages from kids long gone, back to normal school or the Village—their words in permanent marker are all that remain of them now. Curses and insults and other stuff I can't repeat in front of a famous inventor's ghost . . .

"I kinda like the weird graffiti," says Alva. "Like: Right here inside my left armpit I found an amazing message from some girl whom I'll never meet, telling me I gotta keep going. You know? It'll be okay, just keep going no matter how hard it gets. And—well, it's a little private after that. Some things are just between a girl and her left armpit."

"I kinda wish you had more things that were just between you and your armpit, Alva," says Devon.

Alva looks him up and down. "Seven point four," she says. "Keep working on those insults, kid. You really want to be at an eight or nine around here." She turns back to me and Ash. "Sometimes you get a little look at people *sharing* tiny pieces of themselves, you know? This girl could be in college right now, or in jail, or maybe dead. But she was here, and she had a story and a life. That's pretty cool. You're missing some pretty cool graffiti, dude. You should probably be a little more open-minded about stuff."

And with that, she pushes her garbage into her milk carton and shoots it into the trash can on her way out the door. She's so smooth that nobody notices her swipe a handful of grapes with her other hand and sneak them into her pocket. A snack that would be perfect for befriending a certain furry mascot.

The Torture Begins

The lawn behind the school has that fresh-cut–grass smell, and when the tree branches above it shift and flutter, sunlight and shadows play across the field like a swarm of butterflies. The smell of hot asphalt in the parking lot burns in my nose in a nice sort of way, and my lungs fill with this feeling of hope. I close my eyes and concentrate on breathing in and out, and for exactly thirteen seconds I can almost imagine that I'm back in my old elementary school.

But then this crazy music blares from out of nowhere—a trumpet and a full orchestra.

"Okay. What is happening right now?" Devon asks, even more confused than I am.

"Oops!" We hear a woman's voice. "Sorry, everyone! Hold on . . ."

The teacher with the blue shimmer to her hair cuts right

through the middle of our circle without looking up from the remote in her hand.

The music gets louder.

"Just—one moment," she says. "Or two."

Clanging sounds come through the ancient, blown-out loudspeakers in the pavilion—flutes and oboes and xylophones and violins. It's like something you'd hear at a carnival, if that carnival was taking place in a sewage treatment plant.

"Okay! Think I've got it now," she says, and aims the remote like she means it. "Cease this madness!"

The music changes to a mariachi band.

Everyone laughs, but Deadeyes takes pity and sighs. "You want me to try?"

The teacher gives him the remote and when her sleeve lifts I can see those tattooed feathers running up her forearm. Almost as soon as the kid touches it, the music squawks and stops, with one last echo in the silent morning air.

"Whew!" she says. "Much better. Thank you, Mr. . . . ?"

"Jeremy," says Deadeyes.

"Thank you, Jeremy." She smiles and sees us all in a circle around her, staring back at her. "Good morning, everyone! I am Ms. Fitzkopf—Ms. Fitz for short—and I will be your instructor for your first rotation in the discipline."

She continues across the lawn.

"Don't be shy now!" She summons us toward the big

wood-planked pavilion and smiles. "We're gonna have fun today."

"This is some weird new definition of *fun* that nobody else is familiar with, isn't it?" Ash asks me.

I take in the scene at the pavilion, which is *pretty* alarming. There are girls traipsing up and down the length of the planks in rhythm with each other. "You see that?" I ask.

"Oh yeah."

"What are they doing?"

"I don't know," says Ash, "but it's pretty alarming."

This is why we're friends.

Mark is the first to figure out what's about to happen. Because Mark has a sister who takes ballet lessons. "Hey, guys? You're not gonna like it."

"No," says Devon. "They can't do this to us."

"Devon, don't panic," says Mark. "We'll get through this."

"She *can't* be serious," Devon repeats, not really hearing Mark's words. "They're already embarrassing us with these!" He holds his pink arms out at his sides, straight as airplane wings, like they'll contaminate anything he touches.

Ash and I look at each other uncertainly, and turn back to see that Ms. Fitz's eyes have become very bright—filled with a fierce joy that she has stolen right out of our hearts.

"Welcome to the first day of dance class, m'dears!" she says.

Ballet for Bullies

"How many of you are old pros at this?" Ms. Fitz asks. "Hands up if you've ever taken a dance class before."

One hand shoots way up—a kid called Razan who's so tiny and stick-thin that no uniform could possibly fit her. Several other hands follow less eagerly into the air.

"Well," says Ms. Fitz. "That is about to *change*, m'dears."

And so it comes to pass that I learn what a plié is, and a Lindy Hop, and the Charleston, and a whole lot of stuff that I'm not gonna list here because I'm starting to freak out thinking about it all at once, but the point is: I know things. I can never unknow them. And when the demonstration is over and it's our turn to practice, Ash turns to me.

"There's something bothering me, Ian . . ."

"Tell me about it. What part is bothering *you*?"

"Trying to figure out—what's the difference between a ballerina in third position . . . and a superhero who's gotta pee?"

I raise my eyebrows. "I have no clue. What's the difference?"

His face breaks into a grin. "There *isn't* one."

"*What?*" I ask. "How's that?"

And so he starts to paint me a picture of Batman in his super-hero tights, standing in line for the bathroom, waiting and waiting. And he's gotta go bad, so he's crossing his legs and bouncing around on tiptoe, in his tights. *Exactly* like a ballerina.

Suddenly I can see it, and I turn to Ash in complete awe. "You ruined Batman forever."

"Nope. Made ballet awesomer."

But then another idea hits me. "You're right, Ash. It's not a very big leap between the Bat and the ballerina. It's only a tiny jeté . . ."

"A tiny jeté?" says Ash, with a groan. "Why, Ian? *Why?*"

"Because a jeté is ballerina speak for a leap."

He stares at me with an odd look, so I put my arms in a circle over my head and leap as far as my legs can stretch—demonstrating the dance move called a jeté. But I don't quite make it.

Tumbling to the ground, I groan.

"No, Ian. No. I *got* the joke," he says. "It's gonna be part of my brain *forever.*"

"Aww, come on," I complain. "It's a good joke. Work with me, here! I'm trying to make the best of this 'discipline.'"

And so we make the best of it. But our best is very, very bad. It's more like some sort of comedy routine from an old-time black-and-white movie. You know, the kind where people injure themselves in funny ways—where we tell our band leader to "Play us off, Lou!" while we haul our battered bodies offstage to the jangle of ragtime piano, with our boater hats and our red-and-white-striped canes—

In real life we don't have the budget for a full band, though, or canes, or easy access to professional medical care.

"I give up," says Ash. "I don't think we have a future in dancing."

"Yeah. Let's never speak of this again."

"Deal. Never."

"Deny all knowledge."

"Done."

But then we hear a slow, sarcastic clap. Alva Anonymous has been watching us the whole time. "Oh my god, you guys are *terrible*," she says.

"Thanks," says Ash, like it's a huge compliment.

"That looked pretty painful," she tells us. "You want me to get the nurse?"

"No way," says Ash. "We're cool."

"We're totally cool," I agree.

"Not the word I'd use, dude," she says with a slightly amused expression.

"Ian? Ash?" It's Ms. Fitz. "What are you guys doing over there? You're supposed to be practicing the box step."

"Dancing is hard, Ms. Fitzkopf."

She smiles kindly. "Really, Ian, it's not. It's just, you have to be comfortable being you. Okay?"

"Yeah. Okay."

"And you can call me Ms. Fitz."

"Is dancing really a requirement for bully school, Ms. Fitz?" I ask.

"No, Ian, dancing is not a requirement. Dancing is a privilege."

"Can't I just write a report or something?"

Before she can respond, we all turn at the sound of *whoas*—the whole discipline is focused on that movie-star guy with his hair like a helmet. He's doing a break-dance or something, moving like waves crashing on the beach. He's pretty intense, Tom.

And Ms. Fitz is delighted. She claps, loud and proudly. "Oh, we have *another* star!" she says. "Well done, Mr. . . . ?"

"*Rembrandt*," says Razan, with absolute loathing.

She scowls at him for all she's worth, and she's an Olympic-class scowler.

"What do you call that dance?" Cole asks Rembrandt.

Ms. Fitz shoves them together and says, "Cole and Rembrandt. Why don't you two partner up, and you can discuss it while we learn."

"Partner up?" says Cole. "No way, I—"

"It's settled, Cole," says Ms. Fitz. "Everyone else, find a partner!"

When we all freeze, she adds, "If you don't pick a partner fast, I'll happily pick for you!"

With that, the class rushes to find partners, except for Ash and me. We stay totally calm.

"Cool," we say at the same time. Because we're always partners. For everything.

But then I hear a bunch of mean-girl laughter, and I look up to see Miranda's clones smirking as Alva slumps away with a burning blush. Miranda's proud, toothy smile looks like it could swallow any one of us whole—but it's Alva who she's chosen to devour.

"Hey. Do me a favor?" Alva comes toward Ash and me and stops a couple steps away. She takes us in and sighs. "Let me partner up with one of you for this dance thing, okay?"

I can't help but feel bad for her, Tom. Not having a friend here to partner with.

"Come on, *please*?" she presses.

Ash and I look at each other, and we're in total agreement: We turn back to Alva and tell her that we've already got partners. Except that's not exactly what happens. What happens is that Ash says, "Sure, why don't you and Ian be partners?"

I swivel my head back toward him.

"It's cool," he says. "You two go ahead, all right?" He nudges me toward Alva.

"Uh, all right . . ."

But Alva folds her arms and takes a step back. "I'm nobody's second choice," she says.

Oops. "Umm . . . but I didn't—"

And without waiting for me to finish, she adds, "How about it, then, Ash? Wanna dance with me?"

She offers him a hand, and Ash's gaze darts toward her with a smile. "Well . . ."

"Later, Ian," she says. "We'll start over again next time."

"Yeah, all right." *Start over? What does that mean?* I smile even though nothing about this is funny, and then I realize I'm standing there alone. Like the bad old days of being picked last in gym class.

"Ian and Jeremy!" says the teacher when she sees us standing all by ourselves at the edge of the group. "Go on, partner up."

I look over at Deadeyes and feel a flood of anxiousness. He looks back at me with his awful, fiery eyes.

"So . . ." he says.

It looks like he'd rather spontaneously combust than dance a single box step—which is one thing we can agree on, I guess. Maybe there are more things we can agree on, Tom? Probably not.

"Earth to Ian," says Deadeyes. "Anybody home?"

"Not me," I say. "My home is very far from here."

"You got that right, man. Let's get this over with."

"Cool," I say.

"And if you tell anyone about this," he adds, "I will destroy you."

Just at that moment, Miranda screams in pain and that tiny girl, Razan, points right at Rembrandt. "He did it! It was Remy, I saw everything, Remy stepped on Miranda on purpose."

Everyone looks at Remy.

"No way. She who blames it claims it," he says right back. "Tell me somebody saw her!"

Nobody answers. Miranda's angry clones gather around, buzzing like bees and shielding her from Remy and Razan. The battle of wills has been waged—Remy's glance could splinter glass. Razan's glare could blister metal.

"All right," says Ms. Fitz. "Well, we were going pretty good there for a while, at least. You know what? This is a perfect segue into our next session."

"Our next session?" Ash asks.

"Group therapy, m'dear!"

"Oh," he says. "Um, next question: What's a segue?"

She smirks and gestures for us to follow. "Come on and I'll show you."

Remy and Razan

"They're all yours now, Dr. Ginschlaugh," says Ms. Fitz after dropping us in a classroom where all the chairs have been arranged in a big circle.

"Thank you, Ms. Fitz!" booms a voice from inside an adjoining office.

It's that guy who looks like a discount bad guy. Only this time he's wearing a shirt and tie. He drinks us all in and smiles.

"Well then," he says. "Who's ready to talk about feelings?"

It doesn't take long to figure out that group therapy is going to be the most exquisite torture we'll find here at reform school—it's actually people *bragging* about their bullying—but I'm skipping ahead.

"So welcome to group therapy!" our hairless leader announces. "Here, you can say anything you like. The most important rule is to be honest. This is a place for you to be totally honest. *Brutally* honest."

We fidget in our seats.

"Who would like to begin?" he asks with a look around the circle. When he meets my eye, I break out in a cold sweat.

And then he waits, like he's expecting us to read his mind about what happens next. But that's not how classes are supposed to work, Tom—it's the teacher's *job* to tell us about what we need to know for the test. That's why they call them "teachers" instead of, like, "inquisitors."

And still? Much like the Spanish Inquisition, in group therapy the right answers are kept secret. You're supposed to just know them, like by magic, and you're punished with more torturous therapy if you do not.

"Okay, fine," Razan calls out. "I'll go first. You know what the weirdest part of this whole 'discipline' is?" She's pretty dramatic, Tom. "The very first thing they tell us to do here at reform school is the exact thing I did to get *sent* to reform school."

"Hold on," says the girl next to her. "You got sent to reform school for talking about feelings?"

"No." Razan pauses for effect. "I got sent here for *dancing*."

"Oh," says the girl. Then she frowns. "Wait. You got sent to reform school for *what*?"

Razan fires a devilish smile at Rembrandt. He's as far across the circle from her as he can get, I see. And something tells me that's not an accident. "You want to tell the story, Remy?"

"No, you go ahead, Razan," he says, glaring daggers at her. "Tell us a *story*."

"All right, children," says Dr. Ginschlaugh. "Let's get to the point. We'll hear both your sides. Razan, please continue."

Razan's grin gets twice as lopsided, but just when it looks like it'll slide off her face, she brightens and goes on. "Basically it's like this. There we were. Remy and me, I mean." She points across the circle to her nemesis.

He refuses to respond.

"We were the *best*," she says, turning to the rest of the class. "The people loved us and the competition hated us . . . and then Rembrandt ruined *everything*."

Rembrandt rolls his eyes. "Come on—"

"*No interruptions!*" She plows onward: "*There we were*, the champions of the competitive dancing world. Best friends, partners, and there was nothing we couldn't do when we were together . . . *until he betrayed me*."

"Oh seriously! I betrayed you? How did *I*—?"

"You dropped me for another partner, Remy," she explains calmly.

"Your family moved to *Ohio* that year! What was I supposed to—?"

"Oh, I don't know . . . *not* abandon me for a girl who's half a foot short of two left feet?"

"Nice," he says. "You've always been the funny one."

"You know what was *really* funny? When you soaked that kid Luke's costume in dog pee. And when you snipped off half of Daniel's hair so he'd be too embarrassed to get up in front of everyone looking like a—"

"—stop it, Razan. *You* set me up!"

"So you're saying I *forced* you? You were just a helpless, witless idiot?" Her eyes move around the circle defiantly. "That time you replaced Whitney's shoes with ones that were two sizes too small? I somehow tricked you?"

Rembrandt's fists are getting white—and then, after a moment: "What do you want, Razan? We both moved on. You want me gone for good? *Dead*?"

Razan smiles. "Oh, I don't want you dead, Rembrandt," she says sweetly. "But you might *wish* you were after . . ."

"Oh yeah?"

"You know that time you messed up the routine and your mom stood up in the middle of our show and dragged you out of the hotel ballroom while you screeched like a five-year-old with tears running down your face? You might think that was your worst memory, but that will only be the *start* after I've gotten my revenge."

I keep waiting for Ginschlaugh to put an end to it. But he just watches like a reptile, unblinking.

I should probably run away before my turn comes. Or before these two set fire to the room. Or if they don't, maybe *I* should set fire to the room so we can all bust out?

I turn to Ash nervously and he gives me a "calm down" look.

Fine, I promise silently. *I'll stay.*

But in the back of my head, I'm definitely keeping the whole "setting a fire" thing as Plan B.

Starting Over

The next morning when we wake up, all my uniforms are gone. We find them in the bathroom—someone dumped them in the shower and left the water running. Give you three guesses who.

Mark lends me one of his, but it's too big for me.

As I walk into the dining hall, very last and looking like a clown, Cole shoots me a huge smile and thumbs-up. Alva, who's sitting across from him, looks me over from head to toe. "Ian. Your uniform doesn't fit."

"I know," I tell her, majorly annoyed. I thought we were getting to be actual friends.

But when I see her later that day, she's wearing a uniform that's about two sizes too big. "Did someone dump yours in the shower too?" I ask.

"What're you talking about?" she says. "I traded with Lindsay. Gave her half my breakfast for it."

I frown in confusion.

"Kay," she says. "Well . . ."

"Yeah, kay . . . Hold on, why'd you trade?"

She blinks. "The uniform doesn't fit me," she says, like that explains everything. "It's a metaphor?"

"Oh, cool." I have no clue what she's talking about.

"Look . . ." she says. "Ian, you don't have to do that."

"Do what?"

"Pretend like you understand when you don't."

I blush.

"Forget it, dude," she says with a tiny smile. "Let's start over, okay?"

"Start over . . ." I say.

"I mean, that's what this summer is about, right?"

"Starting over?"

"This summer isn't your real life, Ian." She says it like it's the most obvious statement in the world, but it's actually a pretty weird thing to say.

"Well if it's not my real life, what is it?" I ask her, with the sort of curiosity that kills cats.

"It's an experiment. It's another reality, where you don't have to be yourself. You can be anybody you want to." She waits, looking at me with a smile—and then she shrugs: "Or at least that's what I think. Nobody I care about is ever gonna know about anything that goes on in here. So I'm gonna try to figure out some stuff for myself. Especially if I'm forced to hang around total jerks who don't deserve my awesomeness."

And I think about this, but before I can answer, we're interrupted.

"Big E!" Devon bellows. "Reaaaally getting tired of this."

"Who's big E?" says Alva.

"This guy right here. Ian. Big E. And once again, we're all waiting on him to head to stupid dance class."

"Sorry, Dev," I say.

Alva gives Devon a sideways glare. "Don't apologize, Ian. You didn't do anything wrong."

"He's just being nice," says Devon. "Like a normal person. But I forgot: You don't know what being normal is like. Let me demonstrate. 'I'm sorry, Alva, but who are you to butt in on our conversation, anyway?'"

All of a sudden my stomach squeezes. I feel like I'm wearing a really tight belt, even though my uniform pants are still falling down. No, really: I can feel them slip an inch during the moment of dead silence between Devon and Alva Anonymous.

"Well? What do you have to say about that?" Devon pushes.

Alva holds back and just looks at him for a while. And when she does speak, all she says is, "Dude, you do know *Ian* starts with an *I*, right?"

Devon rolls his eyes. "Come on, Hart," he says, expecting me to follow him.

"Hey," I shoot back to Alva. "We'll start over next time?"

She gives me a look like she's not sure what to make of me. "Yeah," she says. "Sure."

"Cool," I say. I feel a huge relief, which lasts almost the whole way through dance class. A new record.

"Oh, come on, it isn't so terrible," says Ms. Fitz. "Very few of you have suffered permanent injury."

We all grumble as we go back and try the whole dance again.

"Though you might take a moment to apologize, if you stepped on someone's foot just now," Ms. Fitz calls over her shoulder.

Something whizzes overhead and there's a skitter of branches and leaves.

"Are we under attack?" I ask.

"It's here," says Deadeyes in an excited hush. "It's really here!"

"What's here?" I ask. "What was that?"

"*That*," says Jeremy, "was a drone, my friend."

"Um . . . like the flying robot kind?"

But Jeremy has already darted into the bushes. He calls back to me, "Ian, if you tell the teachers about this, I swear it'll be my mission in life to make sure you can never go on the Internet *ever* again."

"Tell the teachers about what?"

"I'm serious, Hart!"

"How are you going to stop me from going on the Internet?"

"If you shut your mouth you won't have to find out!"

"Okay, but . . . how can I not tell anyone, if I don't know *what* I'm not supposed to tell them?"

"Ian, stop saying words, okay? This is my advice to you, and I think you should try it."

"I just don't under—*whoaaah* . . ."

And then I stop saying words, because Deadeyes has come out of the bushes carrying something impossible. It shines like a diamond, but it's even better.

"You have a *phooooone*," I say with wonder.

"Stop staring at it. You're getting it dirty just looking at it."

"Where did you—?"

"Everything you're thinking right now," says Deadeyes, "stop thinking it. We gotta get back to practice before Ms. Fitz gets suspicious. And you need to work on your steps. I'm still holding out hope you won't embarrass me out there in front of everyone."

"Not *much* hope though, right?" I ask him.

He frowns. "We have a lot of work to do."

So . . . here's something fun, Tom.

It turns out my partner in dance class is a cyberbully. He's pretty notorious, actually. Made the news and stuff—he went after people online so mercilessly that the FBI *hunted him down*, and because Jeremy was in Canada when they caught up with him, these crazy Canadian Mounties busted down his door and arrested him. He almost wasn't allowed to come back to America.

"Also, you know . . . jail?" Ash reminds me.

He's being super quiet because we're in my bunk and it's after lights-out.

"Yeah, but *Canada*!" I whisper. "Stuck there forever—isn't that sort of cruel and unusual punishment?"

Before he can answer, I go on. "By the way? Don't mess with Deadeyes. He possesses some sort of black magic."

I tilt my head from where we are, lying low in my bunk like spies, to where Jeremy huddles under the covers in his top corner bunk. He's trying to hide the blue glow of an LCD screen from the rest of the dorm.

"Wait," says Ash. "He's got Internet? How'd he get . . . ?"

"That's what I'm saying, Ash."

Black magic's the only logical explanation, Tom. How else could he summon up a shiny new cell phone in this gulag where you have to get special permission to have an electric toothbrush? He's probably chasing down all of our online footprints right now, digging up dirt on us like a starving raccoon spelunking in our garbage.

I seriously hope he doesn't find that potty-training video my mom posted online when I was too little to stop her. You know, the one with the chocolate bar . . .

After Ash climbs down out of the bunk, I carve a single line in the rubbery white paint that's slathered over the cinder-block wall next to my bed. One more day closer to freedom.

To going back to the way things used to be.

* * *

The rest of the week goes by pretty much like that, Tom.

Oatmeal, then dance, then group therapy . . . it all swirls together, like the bottom of a bowl of ice cream.

Every morning, my body is like a rag doll held together with tape and staples and the superstrength snot that comes from a two-year-old having a meltdown. And every morning, I feel like I'm gonna be sick. That's probably why the uniforms are this color: so your enemies can't tell when you puke.

And so I find myself at dinner alone one day, thinking about what Alva said about this not being my real life. The more I think about it, the surer I am that she's right: This is not the same world I was in before I came here. It's a different one. A parallel universe that looks almost like my own . . . but under the surface there are huge changes.

And I close my eyes, and I sit there—and press my fingers into them pretty hard, trying to rub this new idiocy away. Trying to make the world stop spinning. But it doesn't listen.

"Are you okay, Ian?" someone asks.

I know that voice, I think . . . and when I open my eyes and look up to see who it is, my left brain and my right brain lurch with surprise, and trade places, and smash together again.

And I just sort of stare back at him, as if he's some sort of mythological creature. A person from a whole different world.

"Mr. Dunford?"

Community Service

Mr. Dunford stands over me with a dinner tray in his hand.

"Hey there, buddy. Seems like you're having a tough one. You getting the hang of the place all right?"

"Mr. Dunford, what're you *doing* here?"

He looks around the room and then back at me. "I'm on vacation," he says.

"Really?" I ask.

He stands there.

"Oh, I get it," I tell him.

"Never had any doubts! But can I give you a piece of advice? Around here, think a little bit about whatever people tell you—all right?"

"Okay, Mr. Dunford," I say.

"Think for yourself, don't just say okay." He pops a piece of food into his mouth as he speaks. "Mm-mmm! Sweet-potato tots get better every year . . ."

"You come here every year?"

"Sure," he says. "I *vacation* here every summer."

"Oh."

"And by 'vacation' I mean 'teach,' Ian."

"Right."

He claps me on the shoulder and starts away. "M-mm! Hey, don't snooze too long on these tantalizing tubers, guppies!" he advises Miranda's table. "You'll miss out if you wait."

The girls all look at him like he's speaking a language that went extinct because everyone who spoke it kept going insane.

"See you later for second rotation," he tells them.

"What's second rotation?" one of the clones asks.

But Dunford doesn't hear her, because he's singing a made-up theme song called "An Ode to Sweet-Potato Tots."

"Second rotation!" says Mr. Dunford the next afternoon in the classroom where Dr. Ginschlaugh usually tortures us. "It's time to turn the page now. So, whatever you've done to land yourself in this place, it's in the past—and now we will focus on what's ahead of you, okay? Swimming, and surrounding yourself with other people who . . . you know—"

He waves away his words like a cloud of smoke, in a way that's very familiar to me and my friends.

"New things!" he booms on. "Adventures and unexpected experiences and all that. Blah blah blah."

It's nice to have Dunford back.

"So what's next, you ask?" he says. "Well! Let's talk about getting a *job* . . ."

Okay I take it back, Dunford. I didn't miss you at all.

He's up at the whiteboard writing a list or something. Amid the squeak of dry-erase marker, he continues:

"This class is all about understanding your role in the community. Learning to have a positive impact on what's going on in your world. So. Up on the board you'll see several community-service assignments."

He arcs a thumb toward the six available assignments listed on the board, each with a limited number of spaces beneath them. "You will all choose one of these, and it will be your job for the rest of your time here. I know it's a big decision, so go ahead and look at these packets, and take a moment to discuss among yourselves."

Immediately the class erupts into panicked whispers.

"One more thing to keep in mind!" Dunford offers. "All choices are final."

"Okay, okay," says Mark, pulling us into a huddle. "What's our plan here?"

"We should go in for the state park cleanup crew," says Ash. "Reasons? Being outside. Also, the possibility of jumping in a creek. Also, being outside."

"Sounds fun," I say. "But it's gonna be popular—we might not all get to stay together."

"What about volunteering at the county courthouse?" says Mark. I can see the gleam in his eye.

"That's our Mark," says Devon. "Always keeping an eye on the future."

"What do you think we should do, Dev?"

"They all suck," he says. "Do whatever you want. Go make a difference in the world or whatever."

Mark's eyes fall to the floor in embarrassment. "We should stick together, I think."

"Yeah," says Ash.

"We just have to pick a crappy one nobody wants," I suggest.

"Well," says Mark. "I guess a crappy job wouldn't suck so bad, as long as we're all doing it."

"It'll still suck too bad to even consider," Devon says.

"All right, everyone. Time's up! Make your way to the front," instructs Dunford.

We all exchange a look and walk to the front of the room.

"You guys sure about this?" says Mark. "We can't take it back."

Nobody says anything: We just shrug and nod.

"Then it's decided," says Mark. "We're volunteering at the children's hospital."

The next day a bus pulls up in front of the school to take a load of bleary-eyed bullies to their new jobs.

Devon and Mark are whispering in the seat way in the back; Alva and Cole are fighting in the middle; and these three girls who are part of Miranda's clone army but didn't get to tag along with her on her assignment at the state park are grumbling about it, way in the front. I look at Ash expectantly as he quietly pulls out his dad's book—

And the whole mess around us disappears.

Ash and I have been making a game out of reading it when nobody's looking, Tom. We've been trading who gets to carry it each day, and it's probably the best surprise about the whole summer, me and exploring that crazy story with Ash.

We don't say a word the whole bus ride—just duck low in our seat and turn the pages, laughing at all the same places.

And then, when we get to the children's hospital, another surprise: They don't make us wear our salmon uniforms.

"Well now! That's easier to look at," says the nurse who is in charge of us. He exhales in relief at how we look in our new papery, green, poncho-looking hospital uniforms.

"It's less nuclear," Cole agrees—both approving and suspicious.

"What next, Nurse Norse?" says Alva.

Okay. His name isn't really Nurse Norse, but Vikings are called Norsemen, and he's kind of a giant awesome Viking guy, from the way he looks.

As he shows us the ropes, it becomes clear that we're not supposed to do anything, or touch anything, or even ask questions. Basically, we're allowed to deliver mail and take meals to the patients. And we're allowed to breathe—though there have been a few angry looks about us taking liberties with that last thing.

"This hospital is pretty intense, huh?" Mark says to me as we're walking down a long, echoey hall.

"It's confusing," I say. "I'm not sure what we're supposed to do."

"I don't know. We're supposed to think about our 'role in the community' or whatever?"

"Would you keep it down?" a booming voice calls out. "Tryin'a watch my movie here."

I poke my head into the room. This really thin kid with huge eyes made even bigger by these huge, ugly glasses and a long time not being allowed outside is watching a black-and-white movie projected on the cinder-block wall.

"What movie are you watching?" I ask.

"Uh, *Psyyyycho*," he says.

"*Psycho*?" I repeat.

"Film number eighteen in my screening series of Hitchcock's life's work."

I blink at him. "Huh?"

"I'm watching a marathon of all of Alfred Hitchcock's movies."

"Oh. Cool," I say. "Who's Alfred Hitchcock?"

The kid looks shocked. "You've never heard of Alfred Hitchcock? The Master of Suspense?"

I shrug.

"What kind of morons are they sending me?" he asks the vent in the ceiling. Then he swipes some junk off a chair by his bed. "You staying or not?"

I look out into the hall, but Mark is already gone. "Sure . . ."

As I circle the bed to make my way to the chair, spooky music plays while this woman goes into a motel room alone.

Seriously? Big mistake, lady! She's breaking the oldest rule in the book, but before I can open my mouth to say so—

"I know," he stops me. "Just watch. This is important material."

Like usual when people tell me something's important, I immediately black out.

But by the time I open my eyes again the movie's over and I'm still in this kid's room.

"So." My new friend's voice startles me from my rest. "What'd you think of the film?"

"Um . . ."

"Yeah no, I'm just messing with you," he says. "You looked like you could use that nap."

"I was asleep?"

He just smiles. "Viet," he says.

"What?"

"It's my name. What's yours?"

"Ian Hart."

"Welcome to film club, Ian Hart. Feel free to bring a blanket tomorrow if you wanna sleep."

"Sounds great. But I think I have work I'm supposed to do."

"Okay, big shot," he says. "Suit yourself."

But when I catch up with Nurse Norse all ready to make an excuse for disappearing, he tells me something shocking: Apparently my work *is* hanging out with the kids here.

"This is what having a job is really like?" I ask Ash as we're leaving.

"I know! Grown-ups are totally playing us."

The Ruins of a Lost Civilization

"**O**ver here, guppies!" Ms. Fitz sings out. She waves for us to rally around her at the edge of the parking lot. "Your next lesson is off campus," she tells us, gesturing toward the overgrowth disguising a hiking trail in the hills behind the school.

"A hike, *again*?" Ash mutters.

"We don't want a repeat of the first day," adds Mark.

"Okay, enough complaining," says Ms. Fitz. "I think you'll like this lesson."

Miranda folds her arms. "There are probably forty-seven dead bodies in those woods."

"Just hope the murderers are already gone," Alva whispers back.

Miranda rolls her eyes as Ms. Fitz goes on without missing a beat: "Did you know that this place wasn't always a school for bullies?"

Blank faces stare back at her.

"No? Well, it was in your admission packets. You really should read that sort of stuff." She turns on her heel and starts to lead us up the path, her voice carving through the air. "But now you'll have the privilege of hearing *me* tell you the story. The state's best students used to come to study and play here together. To make music, and invent, and write and draw and, yes, even dance."

Our teacher's voice easily carries over us all, expanding on the history of JANUS—and it's kind of interesting. At least compared to the voices in my head.

"You actually had to *apply* to come here," says Fitz. "And guess what? *I* was one of those students—so even now that all of that's only a memory, this place remains very special to me."

Whoa. When I think about her sleeping in my bunk, and sitting at my desk, and wearing these uniforms, all by choice . . . ?

It must've been a way different place back then. Not scary and weird like it is now. And as we tramp along, I try to imagine that it's still like it used to be. I try to imagine that we're all in a special school for talented kids, not a reform school for horrible ones. I pull it off for about thirty-five seconds, before I hear the sound of torture devices.

We stumble out of the woods and into a clearing: right back where the buses dropped us off on that first afternoon.

"Hello, under-fourteens!" says Mr. Dunford. "Welcome to the pride of JANUS! Under-eighteen construction crew, give our friends a proper hello!"

The teenagers are armed with power tools. They mumble at us like zombies as Ms. Fitz brings the class to the top of the hill where we can look down and see what's up here on the hilltop.

It's a stage, Tom.

It's an old, *old* stage, built out of weathered stone blocks. The stage, the seats, the bullies' hearts: all made out of stone.

"What happens up here?" Mark asks one of the older guys.

"The showcase," says the high schooler, heaving big puffs of air as he helps push a piano up the hill. "You know, for parents' weekend?" he adds, like we're idiots. As if *he's* not the one pushing a piano up a giant hill.

"What's a parents' weekend showcase?" Devon asks.

The guy gives up on us and ignores the question, but an older girl wipes her forehead and takes pity.

"You know all those dance lessons you guys do?" she says, her breathing heavy.

"Yeah," replies Devon.

The high schooler gives a pointed look.

"*No way*," says Devon.

"Why don't you show off those sweet moves for us right now?" she teases.

"Come on, kids!" says Ms. Fitz. "Over here!"

I see her waving toward a pile of wood and supplies, and some huge diagrams pinned up on a big easel, fluttering in the breeze.

"We've got everything you need right here. Blueprints, and

wood, and screws—and our under-eighteens have kindly precut and predrilled them for you, all right?"

She looks around at us expectantly. "Well? Any questions?"

Ash raises his hand. "What are we doing?"

"Check out the blueprints."

"But what *is* it?"

She gestures toward the blueprints. "That is up to you to figure out, as a team."

"It's like a puzzle?" says Ash.

He looks at me and I can see he's a little excited.

Ms. Fitz grins right back at him. "Well? *Go!*"

Miranda's minions are off and running before she's done talking. Like any well-trained army, they're good at following orders, and they're halfway done with putting together a sky-high structure by the time the rest of us have even found screwdrivers.

"These things are broken," says Devon. He kicks a pile of boards at his feet. "We need stronger screws."

"Maybe we're missing something," Mark says, staring at the blueprints like they're written in Martian. Our creation is about as much like the thing on the blueprints as potato salad is like ice cream.

"Try a little teamwork, guppies!" says Ms. Fitz. "Why don't you go over there and ask the girls how you can help?"

Grudgingly, Mark brings Miranda to our site to take a look at where we're going wrong.

"No, no, no," she says, taking a mangled mess of half-screwed boards away from Devon. "Do it like this."

She pops two of the boards free and flips them, and they fit together like a fork into an electrical socket.

Mark can't hide how impressed he is as Miranda shows us how to fasten the big sheets of plywood onto the sturdy frame, like in the blueprints. When we see it coming together, suddenly I feel excited: We're building a real thing!

It is a good thing!

I secretly hope that our thing is a catapult.

"It's *not* a catapult, Ian," says Alva.

"How did you know my secret hope?" I ask her.

Ash taps my shoulder. "You said it out loud, man."

Crap.

"This is all scenery for the Parents' Weekend Showcase," Miranda informs us. She shows us how it's going to be a huge, flat thing and how there are all these bright paints waiting to be splattered across the plywood front of it.

My disappointment must be obvious.

"Come on." Alva elbows me. "Let's finish fast and maybe we can do the catapult next."

"Hooray!" says Ash. "I will assemble a list of flingable objects!"

"A long list?"

"Quality over quantity," he says. Then he thinks for a second. "No, you're right: quantity over quality."

"All of the above," I agree.

"Yeah, shoot for the moon!" says Ash.

I laugh. "Shoot for the moon! I see what you did there."

"You guys are extremely weird, you know that?" says Alva.

"We do, in fact!" says Ash.

And just when I'm happily wondering if someone might have pushed the lever on my time machine and flushed us back in time to Old JANUS—the school for the talented kids—that's when I see Devon watching Alva with a heavy scowl.

He spends the rest of the day chucking screws at the tree line.

Cannibal Fish

"Let's just quit," says Devon as we hike back down from the amphitheater.

"We *can't* quit," says Mark. "We gotta do what they say or bad things will happen."

"What bad things, again?" Devon says.

"Well for one thing," says Mark, "if we don't complete the program, they will send us to the Village."

"And for another thing?" Devon asks.

"We will be bullies forever," I say, "and no one will like us."

Devon turns to me like I'm some sort of talking vegetable. Sometimes when he looks at me like that, I think that I might actually *be* a talking vegetable. This is my cue to catch up with Ash.

But just before I get to him, I hear his voice: "Why do people keep calling us guppies?"

"No clue," says Alva.

"Maybe 'cause we're the new kids here?" Ash guesses. "Baby salmon?"

"Good guess. But baby salmon aren't guppies," Alva says.

"They're not?"

"Nope. Guppies are different," she says. "I know because my friend Lacey had a tank full of them in her bedroom."

"Oh yeah?"

"Until her mom flushed them down the toilet."

I shouldn't be eavesdropping on my best friend, Tom . . . but the Freak is way too curious to hear what they talk about when I'm not around, and after wearing myself out in this scorching sun, the Freak's taken over my left arm, three of the fingers on that hand, and both of my legs.

"Her mom *flushed* them?" says Ash.

Alva nods.

"That's horrible."

"That's what I told her! And now I'm not allowed to go over to their house anymore. Because I called Lacey's mom a murderer."

"Whoa, you really called her a murderer?"

"She said they *deserved* it. Can you believe that?"

"Gross," says Ash.

"Yeah! Apart from eating their babies, they're totally innocent."

"Wait. Apart from *what*?"

"It was just *one* time . . ."

"You're joking, right?" says Ash. "This is one of your funny jokes, Alva?"

"Nope. Guppies are totally cannibal fish."

"You're lying," I hear a squeaky voice chime in.

A second later, I realize that the voice came out of my mouth. *Crap.* Alva spins around, eyes right on me. *Double crap.*

"Were you eavesdropping on us?" she says.

"Uh, no."

"Sounds like *I'm* not the one who's lying, Ian," says Alva. "And yes, they're totally cannibals. It's their nature. Also? It's totally uncool that you guys are judging them right now."

"Why's that?" Ash demands.

"How would you feel if *you* got flushed down a toilet because aliens took over the planet and suddenly held you responsible for all sorts of rules you didn't know?"

She has a point. "*Nobody* deserves to be flushed down a toilet," the Freak proclaims and shoots Ash a grin. But Ash doesn't return it.

"You guys have fun with this," he says. "Ian, can I have my book back for a minute?"

As I hand over *The Hitchhiker's Guide to the Galaxy*, I can't help feeling like Ash might be mad at me.

"Sorry for listening . . ." I say.

"Not like we were hiding anything from you." He shrugs. "No secrets between you and me, ya know?"

I swallow hard. "Yeah."

"This place is just messing with us, I think."

"We have to make it home safe," I say.

He manages a smile and then skips ahead to be alone for a little, I guess. But Alva keeps babbling about her friend Lacey's cannibal fish.

"I remember the way they were going around and around the bowl, before—you know . . ."

The way she says it is all dreamlike, like she's weirdly caught in her own head. And the Freak latches on to it and nudges me:

"Hold up," I say. "You *are* lying."

"I told you—"

"*You're* the one who flushed Lacey's fish!"

She looks at me in surprise—and I'm pretty sure she can see the Freak inside my wide-open pupils. "How'd you figure that?"

But I don't want to tell her I've been secretly wondering what she did to get sent here. And I'm not sure how to explain the Freak to her. "So . . . what's going on with you and your friend Lacey?" I ask instead. "Were you bullying her? Is that why you're here?"

For a second she pulls herself up as tall as she can, and I know she's making up a new lie in her head. But then her shoulders droop.

"I don't think Lacey's my friend anymore . . . It's complicated. And scary, and . . ." She opens her mouth and nothing comes out for a second. Like she's reaching for words she can't get her hands on. "You know how sometimes it's hard to make sense of all the crazy pieces in your life?"

I nod.

"Sometimes I just try putting the facts together in a whole different way, you know? Then I kinda start to understand a little better."

"By 'putting the facts together in a different way,' you mean 'lying'?" I ask.

She smirks. A sad version of the thing her face usually does. "Please don't blab about this stuff, Ian."

"I honestly don't understand it enough to blab it. And anyway, I trust you."

"Why would you do a dumb thing like that?"

"I don't think you're that person anymore," I tell her. "We're all bullies here. We all deserve another chance. It's like you always say: We'll start over."

"Those are just words," she confesses. "Lies. All right? I'm a liar."

"Well of *course* you're a liar."

Alva pauses.

"Everybody *knows* you're a liar. You're probably the most honest liar I've ever met though."

Her face stops doing that sad thing, and it makes her look like a whole different person.

"In my experience?" she says. "There are two kinds of bullies in this world: the ones who get caught, and the ones who don't. And you aren't either of 'em."

"What am I?" I ask her.

"You'll figure it out."

Class Participation

"Let's drill a little deeper into your brains today," Dr. Ginschlaugh begins our next torture session.

I can almost hear the whirring of a power tool.

"Let's really *plunge in*," he goes on with a grim sort of joy. "But first? I shall choose today's victim . . . *unless* there's a volunteer?"

A hand shoots up before we've gotten a chance to be terrified.

"Devon Crawford!" says Dr. Ginschlaugh. "You picked a peculiar time to stretch your arm . . ."

"I wasn't stretching, Dr. Ginschlaugh," he says.

"You want to volunteer?" asks the teacher.

Devon nods.

"Well. This is a momentous occurrence! Go ahead, Mr. Crawford. Why are you here with us?"

"I'm here with you because my friend Max had an accident

in the cafeteria one day," says Devon. "As you already know, since Ian can't ever shut up about it for five minutes."

A few bullies smirk and shoot looks my way. I try to ignore the burning feeling in my cheeks and smile back at Devon.

"Let's be clear, Crawford," the teacher says. "Saying it's an accident implies that no one's to blame, but—"

"I know, I know," says Devon. "I fully accept responsibility for the whole peanut butter jam, Dr. Ginschlaugh."

"Good."

"I accept responsibility for everything that happened," says Devon. "I'm used to taking responsibility. To not being able to depend on anyone else. Anyway, I know you all heard a version of the story that made me look like the worst bully of all time, but that's not how it *really* went down. In real life, all I did was what I *had* to do to protect my friends."

"Devon," says Ginschlaugh. "That's not an excuse."

"Sure. Obviously there's no excuse for bullying an innocent kid," says Devon. "But here's the thing . . ."

His eyes scan the room and the next word out of his mouth is full of controlled rage. I can almost hear each synapse firing inside his head, like a rifleman on a Civil War battlefield, as he goes on:

"*Nobody* is completely innocent," says Devon. "All of us have been guilty at some point, and we all need a friend to stand up for us sometimes. Someone who isn't afraid to step in when we're in trouble—"

The teacher clears his throat. "Devon . . ."

"—even if that means being a little bit of a bad guy. You know what I mean, Dr. Ginschlaugh?"

Devon matches Ginschlaugh's gaze. There's a split-second pause and it seems like he and the doctor are battling on a whole other plane.

Like maybe there are invisible arcs of electricity all around us, and these two are testing the other's defenses—and for the first time I think that maybe having a villain's henchman in charge of this discipline is a pretty decent idea . . .

But then Devon laughs like it was all a joke. "Yeah," he says, "I know you understand, Ginschlaugh. That's one of the things I respect about you. You're not afraid to be a bad guy, if it's for a good reason."

Ginschlaugh keeps his eyes on Devon. He smiles in a chilling way. "No. I am not afraid of being a bad guy."

"Neither am I," says Devon. He refuses to be the first to break eye contact. And in that one moment, the way I see Devon changes.

As we file out of the classroom, I get the feeling I am not the only one who sees him differently.

At lunch there's a silence in the air—a danger.

The bullies around us are on edge, like animals before an earthquake, until suddenly a commotion breaks out a few feet away. I turn just in time to see a swarm of girls descending on my table. At the center of the group is Miranda. The biggest bully in the school looks at the four of us and smiles wide enough to swallow us whole.

"Hello, gentlemen!" She puts her tray down on our table. "Mind if we join you?"

Tales from the Cool Table

When Miranda sits down at our table, the entire dining hall of under-fourteens feels a rumble. I look at Ash and ask a silent question—*Was that an earthquake?*

But it wasn't an earthquake. It was just Miranda's tray hitting the lunch table.

"What's your deal, Miranda?" says Alva.

"Oh! Amazing Alva is here too?" says Miranda. "What a nice surprise."

Alva doesn't bother looking up. She just pushes food around on her plate and grumbles, "Don't you have some more girls to brainwash or something?"

"We're actually pretty selective about who we brainwash," says Miranda, without the slightest irritation. "First thing: They have to have actual brains."

Miranda turns back to Devon.

"You know, we were very impressed with your confession," she says with raised eyebrows. "A speech like that, in a school like this? You must be . . . very brave."

"I'm glad someone around here appreciates my work," says Devon.

"Oh. I appreciated every word," Miranda tells him, like it's a challenge or something.

"Good," says Devon. "What's the point of threatening a room full of people if none of them even know that's what you're doing?"

She smiles like a vampire.

"It can get a little lonely, can't it?" she asks. "Not having someone who understands you."

"It can," admits Devon.

"Well. You're not alone anymore."

And Miranda's amusement grows as she and Devon recognize each other as equals. The two of them, completely in tune. Like me and Ash. Only four thousand percent more evil.

Having lunch with Miranda changes some things for the better, if I'm being honest—like how older kids stop "accidentally" splattering milk across our food, or shooting straw wrappers at us when nobody's looking. But some other changes are less than great—like how Devon shoots me and Ash angry looks when we make bad jokes, or how the clones keep pushing us farther and farther down the table. After a while, I find myself just staring at my Jell-O as it wriggles and thinking that I understand exactly the way it feels.

Sitting with the cool kids is no fun, Tom, and it gets worse every meal. This one fateful breakfast, Ash and Alva and I are the last ones stumbling through the food line, and by the time we get to the table, there's only a little room left. A sliver of bench that's barely a butt and a half wide.

"S'cuse me," says Ash. "Could you guys move down a little?"

Nobody looks up.

"Um, guys?" he says.

"Okay, we know you can hear us, clones," Alva growls.

The clones still don't look up.

"You thinking what I'm thinking?" I say to Ash.

"On three?" he says.

And so we slam down our trays and squeeze in at the table at the exact same time, elbowing the clones to make space for ourselves.

Their whines move down the table like dominoes:

"Hey!"

"Eew."

"What're you *doing*?"

But now it's our turn to pretend we don't notice.

"Can I have some of your syrup, Ash?" Alva asks, dipping a waffle without waiting for an answer.

"Look, why don't you sit with someone who actually *likes* you, Alva?" says a clone named Grace.

"This is *our* table," says Alva.

"Right," I agree. "We were here first."

"Were you?" says another clone on the opposite side. "Doesn't *look* like it."

I look up and see Grace staring back at me from a whole different seat.

"Wait," I say. "Weren't you just sitting over there?"

I point back at the first clone and Olivia is there, looking unimpressed. *Ah! Clone trickery.*

"Get it together, Ian," Olivia says.

Then the teacher is there.

"All right, kids," says Ms. Fitz. "What's this now?"

"Alva pushed us out and took our seat," says Grace. "She says it's *her* table. Like she *owns* it."

"Alva?" says Ms. Fitz.

"Come on, Ms. Fitz," says Alva. "You're one of us, aren't you? You know what it's like dealing with . . . the herd mentality."

Ms. Fitz folds her arms. "Alva, if you can't figure out how to deal with people better, you are going to miss out on *a lot* of pretty great stuff in life."

Alva looks shocked at Ms. Fitz. Without another word, she grabs her tray and storms off to a table that's been abandoned due to spilled fruit punch.

"Alva? Wait up," says Ash.

And as he gathers up his food to leave too, I catch Devon's smirk vanishing. He whispers to Miranda, and for a second her expression darkens, but then she waves our way.

"Guys, there's been a misunderstanding, I think," she says. "We can still fit *you*."

She gestures to the table where there are now two pristine, wide-open spaces for Ash and me.

But Ash just turns away, and I follow, joining Alva at the sticky table. For the rest of breakfast, I can feel my neck prickle under Devon's furious gaze. I think it's the most attention I've gotten from him in my entire life.

A Small Favor

On the bus to the hospital, Mark plops into the seat behind me and Ash.

"So," he says, like he's got something on his mind. "I guess we need to talk about what happened this morning."

"I guess so," says Ash. "Because I *never* asked to sit at the cool table."

"I don't like it, either," I agree. "Let's not do it anymore."

Mark goes quiet for a second, thinking. "Okay, look. Why don't you start by telling me what you don't like about it?"

"Did you *see* how horrible they were to Alva?" Ash demands.

Mark nods, calm as a grown-up. "That's why *she* doesn't like it. Why don't *you* like it?"

The way he says it makes me kinda want to puke, but instead of losing my oatmeal I spew out my complaints. "We can't make jokes. We can't be ourselves. We can't *hang out* around all those guys."

"Okay," says Mark. "Is that all?"

I shrug.

"Then I'll take care of it. I'll make sure Devon knows that Ian and Ash are priority number one."

"You'll talk to Devon?" says Ash with surprise.

Mark nods. "Let the horrible jokes begin."

"What's the catch?"

"No catch," says Mark. "But I still need to talk to you about the favor I came to ask . . ."

"And what is this *totally unrelated* favor?" says Ash.

"I need you two to stop hanging out with Alva."

Ash and I wait for Mark to make a joke or something—but he just lifts his eyebrows. "Guys, I'm serious," he says.

"Well, the answer is absolutely not," says Ash.

"Yeah!" I say. "I mean: Yeah we won't, not yeah we will."

"You don't understand," says Mark. "This isn't a debate. You guys *have* to stop hanging out with Alva, and you've *got* to do it *right now*."

"Is this because of Miranda?" I ask.

"No," says Mark.

"Because Alva was our friend first," I remind them.

"We met everyone at the same time," says Mark. "Just because it took longer to get to know Miranda—"

"Devon is out of control," Ash breaks in. "This is turning into the Max situation all over again." He stands up, but Mark drags him back into the seat.

"We're not done talking about this," says Mark.

"Let go of me. I'm gonna go tell him that he needs to quit all this elementary school stuff."

I love Ash. I love Ash so much.

But Mark just shakes his head with a weird little laugh. "Oh, Devon's done with the *elementary* school stuff," he says. "He and Miranda are like . . . *feeding* off each other or something. This morning, when you guys left? They spent the whole rest of breakfast scheming up ways to get Alva sent to the Village."

Tires screech in my brain. "What?" I say.

"Yeah," says Mark.

"No way. They would never . . ."

Mark looks at me. "You *sure* about that?"

"Well, *Devon* wouldn't," I say.

He still just looks at me.

"*Would* he?" I ask.

In the silence that follows, the blood rushes to my ears with a sound like a wolverine gargling, and I glimpse this swirling vision of the future: of Alva being thrown into a jail cell. Of the door going *slam!* and Devon and Miranda looking on with nightmarish cruelty as they sneak a behind-the-back low five.

I feel the desire for a tiny, locked bathroom stall, but keep it to myself.

"Guys," says Mark. "I'm fixing it, okay? I just need you to stop hanging out with Alva so I can tell Devon you stopped hanging out with her. Then I can convince him she's not a threat. Please, just trust me—it'll all go *back to normal* soon."

Ash sighs and I can tell he's thinking about knuckling under. "This *sucks*, Mark."

"I know—you have to do it though. Nobody wants a repeat of what happened to Max, do we?"

"But there's gotta be another way to get Devon to stop," I say.

"Sure, okay," says Mark. "You want to tell the teachers and get him sent to the Village, or should I? Because that's our other option, Ian."

"Look," says Ash, "you don't have to be—"

"No, *you* look," says Mark, as he gets up and climbs down the stairs to the curb. "I'm done arguing with you about this. If you two hadn't left the table today and sat with her over us, maybe none of this would be happening right now."

"You're saying that this is *our* fault?" says Ash, leaping up to follow Mark.

"Who cares whose fault it is?" says Mark. "We just have to deal with it."

We push through the employee entrance of the hospital and down a long hall where we have to whisper because everything echoes.

"Devon's pissed, guys. He's pissed at Alva and he's pissed at *you* for *not* being pissed at her, and I think he's even kinda pissed at me for some reason, which isn't really fair . . ."

"Yeah," says Ash. "You're the real victim here. Life's so unfair to poor Mark Wheeler."

"Guys, come on," Mark says. "I'm *trying* to help her. I'm trying to help everyone."

Ash just shakes his head. "I have to go deliver the mail now," he says.

"Wait," I say. "We gotta figure out a plan . . ."

Ash doesn't even turn around. He just calls back as he walks away. "Yeah, let's *definitely* keep talking about this!"

Mark and I watch him round the corner. "You need to talk some sense into that guy," he warns me.

"Can't you come up with a better way to fix this?" I ask.

"I don't have any other ideas," he says as he starts walking away too.

"But it's what you *do* . . . ," I call after him.

He stops for a second and turns back to me with his arms spread wide. "Do the right thing, Ian! Alva doesn't need you. We do."

Making Things Better

And when I'm standing alone in the hospital hallway, I hear a squeaking sound—it's the saddest sound in the entire universe, and it makes me want to start laughing. I turn to see a kid emerge from his room, pushing a cart ahead of him with a bunch of cables dangling from it. For a second I think it's some big medical contraption, but then I realize it's his movie projector.

"Viet?" I say.

"Ian!" He powers on, heaving with exertion just from walking.

"What're we doing today?" I ask as I help him steer the cart down the hall.

"I wasn't gonna bother you with it. I overheard what you and your friends were arguing about."

"I could deal with being bothered," I tell him.

He brightens. "Well. I'm heading to the dayroom. And I'm

attempting to hack together a home-brew 3-D screening of Hitchcock's *Dial M for Murder*."

"Seriously?" I say. "That's awesome."

"You have no idea what that is, do you?"

"No."

I help him set up the dayroom like a theater, with all the chairs in rows, and all the sunshine sealed out so it's pitch-black when the lights go down—which is a little confusing to the half-dozen other kids who are in there with us. Viet promises they're in for a treat and they ignore him, like this isn't the first time they've heard that promise.

"So, before—you heard everything?" I ask him.

"Couldn't help it," he says. "It seems . . . pretty screwed up."

I just laugh. "I can't deal with it anymore, Viet."

"The only thing you can't do is drink an entire gallon of milk at once."

"Or eat a whole teaspoon of cinnamon," I say back.

"Or stay awake through an entire Hitchcock movie," he teases me.

"Hey, I woke up for the end of that one."

"Which one?"

"Where the guy's hanging from the end of President Lincoln's nose."

"You mean from Mount Rushmore? *North by Northwest*?"

"Yeah, that."

"You didn't even *get* the ending," he scoffs. "I had to explain it to you."

"Whatever, it was dumb the way it ended."

"Dude!" says Viet. "Hitchcock was making a *comment*—wait, you're messing with me now, aren't you?"

I grin. "It's fun when you get all worked up."

He drops his head and mumbles, "Hitchcock is a genius."

"You'll be way better one day, Viet," I say. "Your movies will actually make sense. Or at least they'll all be in color, anyway."

"It's time to go, Ian," Nurse Norse calls before I know it.

"Already?"

"Ash, you too," the nurse motions across the room.

And that's when I see Ash hiding in the corner, playing this card game the older kids taught us at JANUS. It's a game called slap where you have to slap a pile of cards really fast, and sometimes it gets kinda intense.

This game isn't intense, though. Ash is just showing a younger girl the ropes.

"Aw, man!" she says when Ash points out that she forgot to slap the double sevens.

"Well, let's go ahead and slap on the count of three," he says.

Her face turns into a huge grin. "One," she says. "Two—" And before she gets to three, she slaps. "Mine!" She scoops up all the cards.

"Nice one!" says Ash.

She scowls. "Are you going easy on me?"

"Yes," he says.

"Don't go easy!" she complains.

"You just find some more kids and practice while I'm gone," says Ash. "And tomorrow, when I come back . . ."

"Sweet vengeance!" she roars.

Ash looks up at me with a big grin. "I taught her that," he says.

"It's pretty great," I reply.

And then, as we're walking back, I feel my feet getting heavier. And heavier. And maybe I slow down a little . . .

"I know," says Ash. "Is it weird that I want to stay in the hospital instead of going back?"

"No," I say. "Wanna see if we can hide out?"

"What about Alva though?"

"Oh yeah."

"Ian. What're we gonna do?"

"Do you think Devon would *really* get a kid sent to the Village?" I ask.

We walk toward the bus in silence, and Devon and Mark come up from behind and hurry past, joking like everything's fine.

That's when Ash makes his decision: "Listen. I'm not letting anybody bully me into not sitting with my friend. Let alone someone who's *also* supposed to be my friend."

"Well," I say after a moment, "then this is going to be fun, isn't it?"

Return of the Cool Table

"**M**mm, looks great tonight, right, guys?" says Mark as he follows way too closely behind Ash and me through the food line in the dining hall. He sticks to us like glue, hurrying us over to our still-empty table.

"And here we are," Ash says drily.

"Safe and sound," I agree.

Ash and I look at each other, and at the same time, we move apart to save a place for Alva in between us.

Mark goes rigid. "I thought we had a plan, guys."

Before he can argue, Ash calls out to Alva and points to the seat next to him.

"Hey, guys," she says, walking up to the table.

And then she blows straight on past us without even slowing down.

"Hey! Where're you going?" says Ash. "We saved you a space."

"No thanks, I'm good. Cole saved me a seat tonight."

She nods to the Stachesquatch across the dining hall.

"Oh," Ash says.

"Wait," I say. "Since when isn't *Cole* sitting with *us*?"

Alva's mouth quirks upward. "Have you really not noticed that he got squeezed out like two days ago?"

Ash and I look at each other. Has Cole been sitting alone for the past two days? As I'm trying to figure out how I didn't notice that, Alva gives me a thin-lipped smile.

"Have a super *cool* dinner, you guys," she says, and turns away.

"Hey, come on!" pleads Ash. "We want you to stay, Alva."

"Yeah, Cole can come too," I say. "Come back and hang out!"

Just then Devon arrives with his taunting voice: "Yeah, Alva! Come back—we *really, really* want to hang out with you."

I burn with embarrassment as she scowls at us and makes a gesture I cannot describe in front of a famous inventor.

And then I feel Devon slide into the seat between me and Ash. He smiles hugely at us. "Thanks for saving me a seat."

I keep watching Alva as she eats her dinner, laughing and talking with Cole. Their presence appears to totally annoy the other guy at their table—Deadeyes, who always eats alone and pretends to read a book, while secretly using his phone.

"Okay, seriously," says Devon. "Are you even paying attention?"

"Huh?" I ask. I guess he's been talking to me.

Devon stares. "I thought we were gonna hang out, Ian. Didn't you want to tell jokes? Isn't that what you told Mark? That you were sick of being ignored or whatever?"

"What?" I ask lamely.

Devon gets frustrated. "Dude, what is going on with you?"

"I'm sorry. I just—I'm not feeling good, I think."

He frowns at me and throws his hands in the air like he gives up. "Whatever," he says, grabbing a handful of sweet-potato tots before rising to his feet.

"See ya later," he says, already halfway to the other end of the table. Miranda's side.

I look over at Cole and Alva, and Mark grips my shoulder.

"Don't do it, Ian," he says. "It's fixed. Just leave it."

"I just want to go over for a minute and talk to her," I say. "Tell her why we're being weird."

"Why would you stir things up right now?" he whispers in frustration. "She's *happy* over there."

I look at Ash. But he shakes his head no too.

"He's right. She didn't even want to sit with us. Leave her alone."

He stares at his plate and pokes his half-eaten food, like he's just been told that the sauce on his spaghetti is actually dog barf.

"Be a little easier on yourselves, guys," Mark says with a small smile. "You can't solve every problem."

I flick my gaze sideways like I'm slinging a water balloon at him. Mark dodges out of the way.

Inside my head, the Freak is fired up. And as much as I fight against it, before long I'm thrusting my legs against the ground and lurching out of my seat.

"What are you doing, Ian?" says Mark.

"I am going over there before this gets out of control," the Freak announces. "No one try to stop me!"

Probably because they're really surprised, nobody makes a move to grab me. I walk over to Alva's table so quickly that the Freak and I don't have time to figure out what we want to say.

Cole and Alva slowly raise their heads.

"Hi, Ian," says Cole.

"Hi, guys?" I say, somehow making it into a question.

"Whatcha doing?" Alva asks.

But I'm frozen. Standing there with my mouth hanging open and no words coming out. And then? As may happen when you let your mouth hang open, something flies into it, like a plane landing at the airport . . . only its runway is alive and definitely doesn't want to be landed on. I start to cough, trying to spit out the bug or whatever flew into my mouth.

Everyone is staring.

And the next thing I know, the Stachesquatch is thumping me on the back over and over, and I cough up something weird: a little pellet of paper.

A spitball. A sharpshooter shot right into my mouth.

I try to look around for the shooter, but Cole is still thwacking me on the back. Whacking the air out of my lungs.

"Stop!" I wheeze at him. "Stop, I'm fine. Cole!"

"You alive?" he asks.

"Gentlemen!" says Mr. Dunford, coming up behind us. "What's going on here?"

"He's hitting me," I complain.

"*Hitting* you?" says Cole. "I was saving your life!"

"Looked like you were choking pretty bad to me, dude," Deadeyes pipes up, suddenly distracted from his phone. "Ooh! Ian, you totally owe him a life debt now."

"Ooh!" Cole echoes. "Yeah, you have to follow me around and do what I say forever."

Mr. Dunford decides to let the matter drop. "You okay, Ian?" he asks, quietly. I give him an embarrassed nod.

"Good," he says. "Have a seat, then."

For a moment he leaves a comforting hand on my shoulder. It only makes me feel worse. I look super pitiful right now, and I'm clearly not fooling anybody.

As Dunford walks away again, my eyes flick toward Alva to see what she's thinking about all of this.

Which is when I realize that she's gone. Vanished, Tom. Like snow when you step inside the house.

"Ah, crap," I say.

"You choking again?" says Cole.

He winds up to start hitting me again.

"No, *no*—where did Alva go?"

Cole and Jeremy point to where she's heading out of the dining hall, and I'm about to chase after her when there's a commotion at Devon and Miranda's cool-kid table. I see them leap backward with an "Ugh!" as a bottle of soda explodes like a fire hose, drenching the entire table in sticky brown liquid.

"Who did that?" Mr. Dunford turns back to face the room.

For a second, there's no response. Then just a single, small voice:

"It was Alva, Mr. Dunford," says Ash. "I saw the whole thing."

Everyone's head swivels to Alva, who pauses in the doorway and looks back at Ash in shock.

Devon and Miranda's expressions go from completely grossed out to wide, wide grins.

"Ash and Alva?" says Mr. Dunford. "Judge Cressett's office, please."

Ash's Secret

After dinner, a group of boys settle into a game of slap on the floor in the dorm, but the game ends and begins and ends again and Ash is still in the Judge's office.

He comes in right before lights-out, and Devon cheers for him like he's a hero, clearing room in the circle for him to sit. But Ash climbs up into my bunk and sits with me instead. Staring into space.

"You okay?" I ask him.

"How do you know if you're doing the right thing?" he asks.

". . . asking the wrong guy," I say.

He swings his head around toward me. There's a little laugh in his throat, but it doesn't make it the whole way to his mouth. "Everything's screwed up," he says. "But at least *they* won't try to get her kicked out now."

For a minute, I just sit there—and then I shake my head. "Only *you* could make being the bad guy a selfless act."

Ash's eyes are full of guilt anyway. "She hates me now."

I don't know what to say to that.

"I'm gonna go read, okay?" says Ash.

I nod, and he starts to climb down. But he pauses on the ladder and thinks again.

"Actually. There's something I need to tell you," he says.

"About what?" I ask.

He climbs up again. "Remember when Devon slipped Max that peanut butter?"

I feel a little chill. "Sure."

"He *knew*, Ian. About Max's allergy."

"Yeah," I say. "He thought it'd make Max sneeze."

At Ash's expression, I feel the chill tighten around me.

"No. He knew how dangerous it was for Max."

I feel a giant, icy thing gripping me.

"And I warned Max to be careful," Ash goes on. "That Devon might try something like that. So he wouldn't fall for it."

I feel the sinking, swirling beginning of a *flush!* and force myself to hold firm right in the moment where I am. "But if you warned him, then why did Max fall for it?"

Ash shakes his head. "He didn't want to lose us as friends. He thought Devon wasn't that evil—"

I feel the *flush!* coming closer, like a storm rolling in . . .

"He thought you were cool, dude. Me and you. So he hung in there through it all."

I sit with Ash and feel like I'm just a tiny speck in a stormy ocean of a toilet bowl. I paddle to keep my head up. "And every-one knew it was happening but me?" I ask.

Ash shrugs.

"Motto of my stupid life," I mumble.

Ms. Fitz's voice calls "LIGHTS OUT" from the hallway and everyone starts to scamper through the darkness like well-trained cockroaches.

"Ash?" I whisper in the flurry of motion. "We said no secrets. Why didn't you tell me before?"

"I've been wanting to . . . but . . ."

Then I figure it out. "You were protecting me."

He looks back up at me from the ladder. "Did it work?"

"Two point six."

He climbs down leaving me staring at the dark ceiling, all the stuff about Max swirling around my mind . . . and I pull the covers over my head, trying to block it all out and avoid get-ting sucked into the cosmo-flush.

But there's a big flaw in this plan. Maybe the best way to put it is . . . well, you know what happens when you flush a toilet but it doesn't go down, Tom?

Exactly.

I lie there in horror as the toilet-time machine belches up more and more rotten memories. As all the disgusting guilt and fears flood over the edge, pouring on and on and on.

But even late at night, I better not stop pretending to be brave. Not in a room full of monsters. So I heave off my covers and climb down my bunk to go to the one place I can drop the act. But before I get there—

"What are you doing out of bed, Mr. Hart?"

I turn. "Mr. Dunford?"

"Are you feeling okay, Ian?"

"Can't sleep."

He nods. "You know what the best thing about insomnia is?"

I shake my head.

"It's the snacks."

"The snacks?" I ask.

"The snacks. For insomniacs."

I feel a little tug at my mouth. "Insomni-snacks?"

"Indeed," he says.

He leads the way to the kitchen pantry and lets me sit at the table in the middle of all the shiny metal appliances and the dirty gray light from the lonely fluorescent lamp above.

"Let's see what there is." He rummages through the shelves and pulls a can of sliced peaches and a bag of pretzels from the stash. "Take your pick."

He doesn't ask to talk. He doesn't make me listen. There's just the crinkling of a bag, and the hum of the giant refrigerator thrumming through the night.

Swimming Upstream

The next morning, Ash and I barely say a word at breakfast. We just stare at our food while the cool kids laugh on and on at Devon and Miranda's jokes. The two of them are an unstoppable force now. I'm pretty sure they found a cheat code that makes them invincible, even though the rest of us are stuck on the same level—with the difficulty all the way up to Impossible. It's like we've been taking so long getting to the final boss that it's gotten bored from waiting: It just comes out to stomp us in the middle of the game and drop-kick us the whole way back to the beginning, taking our power-ups too.

Ash and I keep slogging along, barely managing to keep up with the rest of the group, while Devon and Miranda are actually having *fun*. Like, on the hike to the hilltop when they're sneaking around, and Devon makes this little side-step across the trail right before Razan face-plants on the ground.

Well, almost face-plants. Let's not forget who we're dealing with: As soon as she loses her balance, Razan turns the fall into a somersault and propels right back to her feet.

"Rookie move, Rembrandt." The conspirator-clones have already closed in around Miranda and Devon.

Razan shoves Rembrandt with some sort of secret dance-based martial arts move, and he stumbles into a thorny bush.

"Real mature, Razan." He reappears, shaking burrs from his perfect hair and needles from his clothes.

"You wanna start this now?"

"Start it? This has been coming for a long time," he says. Then he swipes out at her with a leg and suddenly they're a blur of movement before Remy ends up flat on his back. As with most ninja fighting, their battle lasts six seconds at most. Too stealthy for the teachers to notice.

"Had enough?" she asks.

He looks up at her, breathing heavy but just getting started. "To be continued," he says. "Later, in private."

"Much better idea," says Razan.

Rembrandt scowls. "Then why'd you start it here, unless you *wanted* an audience?"

"*You* started it," says Razan.

"What're you talking about? You just treed me out of nowhere."

"After you tried to make me eat dirt!"

"I did not," says Remy, and there's a weird, wounded look on his face. "As if *I'd* ever think *you* could be taken down by being tripped."

"Then how . . . ?"

She stops and, in the silence, a tiny snort escapes from the army of clones.

"Hooold on," Razan tells Remy.

She wheels toward the clones as they try to stifle their laughter, yanking girls aside until she's face-to-face with Miranda and Devon. "I want to thank you two."

Miranda smirks. "For *what?*"

Razan doesn't answer. She just turns away from Miranda and grabs Remy by the front of his shirt, hauling him along behind her. "Rembrandt, this little feud has been a lot of fun and everything, but we have something more important to do."

"Uh. Yeah?" says Remy.

Razan nods fiercely. "Unite to destroy Miranda and Devon."

"You mean we're getting the team back together?" he asks. "Well it's about time!"

And just like that, Remy and Razan's feud is ancient history—even as, on the far side of our salmon-colored infestation, Ash and Alva's is just beginning.

"Are you gonna avoid her for the rest of the summer?" I ask at the beginning of group therapy.

"Maybe. I don't know . . . I just need some space, you

know?" says Ash. "Not all of us can keep it together as easy as you do."

But he sounds sort of jealous, and it makes me laugh.

"You think I'm keeping it together? You have got to be kidding."

"You just keep *going*," he says, totally sulking.

"It's not—it's all an act, dude."

"No it's not. You're really brave. It's really annoying."

I look at him like he must be telling a joke I don't understand, but there's no hint of it in his expression.

"Ash, I—"

"*Good morning!*" Dr. Ginschlaugh booms, slamming the door. "Quiet down, please. Let's begin."

He plops into the chair next to Ash and asks for a volunteer like usual, but as he does it, he scribbles on a scrap of paper and drops it into Ash's lap.

Ash reads it with a frown, and then embarrassment. And his eyes flit up to meet mine. He sort of laughs, and passes me the note.

It says: *What's the difference between* acting *brave and* being *brave?*

I watch him thinking about this, and I know I need to help Ash fix things with Alva. I spend the rest of group therapy thinking of a way to get him to talk to her, but I know Ash wouldn't do anything to make her a Target for Devon and Miranda again. And he's probably one of the most stubborn people I know. Especially when he's got a good point. So I decide to try something else: tell Alva what's *really* going on. I wait until the moment after dinner, when everyone at my table has fallen into food comas, and I catch up to her outside the dining hall.

"Alva!" I call out. "Wait up."

"What do you want, Ian?"

"Could you slow down? I wanna talk to you."

She doesn't answer.

"Where are you going?" I ask.

"More about what I'm leaving behind," she says without looking back.

"Alva, come on . . ."

She's right at the door to the girls' dorm now. "No," she says, and pushes inside.

I catch the door before it closes and prop it open with my foot. "We gotta talk."

"Ian." She's totally exasperated. "You're not allowed inside here."

"I'm not technically inside."

I try to avert my eyes in case it helps my case—but after two seconds, the Freak gets really curious and forces me to look around. There isn't a huge difference between the way the boys' dorm looks and the way the girls' dorm looks, Tom. But there is a big difference between the way they *smell*. The boys' dorm smells like old sweat and gummy bears, and the girls' dorm smells like crushed grass and sunscreen—but now I'm getting distracted.

Through it all, Alva is watching me like a thunderstorm eyes a tall tree. "Your friends are not *technically* buckets of sewage," she says, "but I think we're past technicalities, don't you?"

I look at my feet, hoping to diffuse the storm, or maybe find some brilliant words down there on the ground.

"Don't you dare act like a puppy, Ian."

"Sorry, I'll leave. I just—forget it. Sorry."

"Oh my gosh!" she cries. "If you're capable of bursting in here, then you don't get to play sweet and innocent. Just say what you need to say and then we can all go back to being forlorn at literally everything."

"Go back to being what?" I ask.

"Are you coming in or not?"

My legs respond without even checking with me—and there I am, inside the girls' dorm.

"Speak. Let's get this over with."

"I just wanted to tell you that . . . that Ash didn't really mean to get you in trouble. He was trying to help."

She gives a mean little laugh. "You spend an awful lot of time telling people what your friends really mean, you know that?"

"I'm saying that you don't know the whole story."

"Ah, so I have no clue what I'm talking about?"

I try to answer, but my mind has gone blank again and she keeps going. Seriously, how do other people always know what to say faster than I do?

"Here's the truth," she says. "Your friends are jerks. And they're making friends with even worse jerks—which makes it seem pretty likely to me that you're deep down a jerk too."

I stand there awkwardly. "I really like hanging out with you, you know."

She doesn't budge.

"So does Ash," I add. "Even though everything that's going on has been a little confusing."

"Yeah, it is confusing," she says. "The way you say 'we' and 'us' all the time. You and Ash lump yourselves together with Devon and Mark—and now *Miranda*—and so after a while it just . . . Who *are* you, Ian?"

"I just wanna make things right," I tell her.

"I believe you. And I *know* you're trying your best. The problem is—I just don't care that much anymore."

It feels terrible, hearing her say she doesn't care. And in that moment, I realize how much I *do* care. And I open my mouth to tell her that, but what comes out is: "He always protects us, Alva."

"What?"

"*Devon*," I say. "He always—he's just always looking out for me. He's always on my side, no matter what. You know?"

"Does he ever *listen* to you?"

"He doesn't listen to anybody," I complain. "That's not—look, here's the thing. After I met him, I was never worried about . . . being the one who got left out. Who ended up alone."

"Here's a secret, Ian," she says. "There are worse things than being alone."

And without giving me the chance to say anything back, she walks out, leaving me standing in the under-fourteen girls' dorm.

I rub the heel of my hand into my eye until it's painful and the pain keeps me from floating away.

And when I get back to my bunk, I know I'm not the only one in this personal prison.

"Ash?" I whisper.

Ash is in his bed, sobbing.

"What happened?" I ask.

He looks up and I can see him holding something against his stomach. It's his dad's book—*The Hitchhiker's Guide to the Galaxy*—and I can tell something's wrong with it even before he gives it to me.

Ash's face crumples and his eyes start getting all glassy again. He crawls farther into his bunk and faces the wall.

I open the book with horror . . . and then fury.

It's sixty-four slices of American cheese, squashed between every page.

The Cheesening

Ash's dad's book had been in the family since he was our age, Tom.

His fingers turned the pages a thousand times, you could tell from reading it. And he had drawn all these cartoons in the margins that made his favorite scenes even better. He trusted Ash with that book.

"I'll find whoever is responsible," says Devon as we're on the way to dance class the next morning, muddy from digging a woodland grave for *The Hitchhiker's Guide*.

"Like we don't know who it was," Ash says.

"You think you know who did the Cheesening?" I ask.

"Come on, it has to be Alva," he says with a gesture to where she stands making jokes with Cole.

"What about Remy and Razan?" I ask. "They were mad—"

Ahead of us the Rs are dancing together like the champions they once were. I've never seen them so on their game.

"I guess bully school is really working out for some people, huh?" Ash spits out.

"Ash—"

"You think they're happy 'cause they're the ones who just got away with something?" he asks.

"I think they're happy because they're friends again," I respond.

"Yeah, me too," says Ash, like he was hoping for another answer.

"Good for them," says Miranda, with grudging respect.

Devon looks at her in shock, but Miranda keeps her eyes on the Rs. "Man, I wish I could dance like that," she adds with a hint of jealousy.

"Do you dance and stuff?" Devon asks.

"I'm the biggest klutz ever. But gimme an instrument if you want to see what I can do."

Well now I'm curious. "Which instrument do you play?" I ask.

"Whichever," says Miranda.

"Just . . . whatever's lying around?"

As she's talking, Ash pulls Mark to the side. "If it wasn't the Rs, guess that leaves our one main suspect, huh?"

Mark shakes his head. "Don't jump to any conclusions. We don't know anything for sure."

"But you're checking it out, aren't you?" says Ash.

"Cole thinks he *might've* seen Alva sneaking into the kitchen."

"Right," says Ash. He doesn't need any more proof than that.

Remy and Razan finish their dance with a swoopy-thingy, I think is the technical term, and as Razan lands on her feet, Ms. Fitz claps fiercely.

"Brilliant!" she tells them. "You two are an amazing team. Reminds me of the old days, watching you. And as a reward for all your hard work, I want to do something special. Class, meet our new *co-choreographers* for the Parents' Weekend Showcase!"

"*Really?*" says Razan.

"Let's give our stars a round of applause!"

Above the sound of the four people who decided to clap, Ms. Fitz goes on, "Now, the showcase is this weekend—it's time to get serious."

Jeremy leans close to me. "This means you, Ian. You're not gonna embarrass me out there, are you?"

"I make no promises."

"Ian," says Jeremy. "You may not have realized this yet . . . but this showcase is a *real* thing that is *really* happening. And there will be an audience. And there will be people in the audience— terrible, terrible people who are going to *record* it."

"You mean . . . video?" asks Ash.

"This is a dance recital, dudes," Jeremy says. "Someone's *definitely* gonna record it."

I realize he's right.

"High-definition, slow motion, possibly a virtual reality simulation—embarrass yourself and it's gonna be your number one Google result forever."

I moan. "Jeremy . . . I'm hopeless."

"I know. That's why I got you some help, *partner.*"

He beckons across the class, and Remy and Razan come over. Our new *co-choreographers.*

"Why don't you show us what we're working with here?" says Razan.

I smile thinly at them and pull Jeremy away. "Look," I say. "It's really nice of you, but—"

"I don't think you understand," Jeremy interrupts. "My hacker enemies will turn this into a meme. No! My hacker *friends* will turn it into a meme. My *enemies* will never be able to take me seriously again. I had to *beg* the Rs to work with us."

I bury my head in my hands. "Jeremy, between this and Devon and Ash's book and—"

Jeremy cuts me off. "I'll make you a deal."

"What sort of deal?"

"Listen to the Rs, learn the dance—and I'll use my unique skills to investigate your cheese treason. See if Alva's really to blame."

I sigh, and resentfully pull Jeremy into our little dance routine. But halfway through, Razan has her head in her hands.

"You're not even watching, Razan!" I complain.

"She's always been the smart one," says Remy. His eyes are wide like he's just seen a snake swallowing its dinner.

"So," says Jeremy. "Do you think you can fix him?"

"It would be our greatest challenge."

"Or our finest achievement."

"You guys," I say. "I'm standing right here."

"Good," says Remy. "Stand as still as you can. Moving, for you, is a very dangerous business. I'm amazed you've survived this long outside of full-body bubble wrap."

"So tomorrow?" says Jeremy.

"Dawn," says Razan.

"Come hungry."

"But eat a good breakfast first."

We practice hard all morning, Jeremy and me and the Rs. It doesn't seem to be doing any good, but during one of our breaks I catch Alva watching us from across the class. Her eyes dart away from mine and that's when I notice Ash is standing beside her, yelling.

"Look, if you didn't do it, then just say it wasn't you," he demands.

"I can't believe you're even *asking* me about this," Alva says.

Ash snorts. "You sound so guilty right now."

"How do you figure *that*?"

"You won't even *deny* it."

"And I won't even dignify that with a response," says Alva.

"Saying you won't respond is totally a response!" says Ash. "Dignity acquired against your will!"

She looks at him, somewhere between offended and disappointed, and slumps away in her twice-too-big uniform.

What if she wasn't the person who ruined Ash's book, Tom?

I turn toward Mark, who's looking uncharacteristically stunned. "What if we've got it all wrong?" I ask him.

He crumbles a little. "I've been wondering that myself."

Hacked

The night before parents' weekend, Jeremy pulls me aside. "I have an answer for you about your little book situation, Ian."

"And?" I ask.

His expression darkens. "I'm just gonna show you."

"You're gonna show me what?"

He weighs his phone on his palm. "Video from the security system in the dorm room."

"There's a camera watching us sleep? Gross."

"Yes. And yes."

Jeremy's jabbing and swiping and speeding through the video of an empty dorm room, looking for the right spot.

"So—did you hack into the mainframe or something?"

"No."

"You installed a worm in the cloud?"

He looks up and studies me. "Ian—focus, okay?"

"I'm just interested."

"It was a spoofed KinderCorp e-mail account and a little bit of social engineering. Feel better now?"

"I'm even more confused, actually."

"Imagine my surprise."

Jeremy hands me his headphones and presses Play. It's our bunks, as seen from the upper corner of the room. And there are two people in the room. One at Ash's bunk, and the other one watching the door. I squint, but I can't make them out.

"Who is it?" I ask.

"Wait for it."

I keep watching. I watch the Cheesening happen in real time. It's like the time machine: I can see it happen, but there's nothing I can do to stop it. Then I hear a voice:

"Hurry up. Someone's coming!"

That's when I recognize who's on guard at the door. It's *Mark*.

I go rigid and look up at Jeremy—

"Keep watching," he says.

I look back down as the other guy is talking: "Not yet, not yet! I've got like half a pack of this left still."

Jeremy's gaze flits up at me, waiting for my reaction. The other guy is Devon, of course. And I feel a buzzing in my ears as he lets out this excited giggle that makes me want to spew.

"Turn it off, please."

Jeremy pulls the phone away. "I'm sorry, Ian."

I manage a nod.

"What're you gonna do?"

"Does Ash know?"

"No, I just got hold of this. And *you* are the only one I'm gonna tell—but this knowledge comes with one condition."

"A condition?" I say.

"You can't tell anyone what I showed you until tomorrow, okay?"

"Why?"

"Because I want to be far, far away when word gets around to your friend Devon that I gave you that video."

"They're letting you go?"

He shakes his head and grins. "I'm busting out, actually."

"Seriously? What'm I going to do without a partner for the showcase tomorrow?"

"Ian, come on. You physically *cannot* do any worse than you already are. You're the main reason I have to get out tonight."

Can't argue with his point. "So where are you going?"

"Canada. The Collective has a plan to bust me out."

"The Collective?" I ask.

"You don't want to know about the Collective, Ian. It's not safe for you to know about them."

"But—"

"Aren't you in *enough* trouble?"

I frown.

"No, you definitely don't want to know about the existence of a group of brilliant, ruthless hackers that secretly controls two continents . . . because if you *did* know about them, you'd never be safe again."

I don't know what to say to that. But he doesn't seem to be paying attention.

"So anyway," he goes on, "I'm putting this video on a website I set up for you, and I'm making the password Ontario, and I'm walking away. It's up to you to do whatever you want to do with this information."

On his phone, a little spinning icon pops up with a cheery little *I did it!* sort of sound.

"Good luck, Ian."

And that's the last I'll see of old Deadeyes, I know. For better or worse, he's done with JANUS. But he's still out there. Beyond my knowledge. Beyond his teachers' control.

If anybody in this story takes after you, Edison, it's surely that guy.

There is a message scratched into the wall of the time machine at JANUS. Five words carved with loving violence:

We are the real monsters.

It always made me shiver a little, seeing it there—and now, when I see it tonight, I get this weird idea that it's a message that I went back in time to tell myself in the only way that I knew how: by scratching it into the wall of a place I knew I'd find.

In the end, we're all just guppies. Cannibal fish. Mark and

Devon aren't really on our side, and we betrayed Alva when she needed us too.

And what will happen when I tell Ash about Mark and Devon's sixty-four slices of betrayal? Is he going to be even more broken up? What if I just go on letting him think it was Alva who committed cheese treason? Didn't he protect me from having to deal with the truth about what happened to Max?

But . . . it would have been better if he'd told me about Devon at the beginning, wouldn't it? I'm not going to hide the truth from him now. I'm sick and tired of feeling helpless.

And I'm not even sure if it's me or the Freak that's spoiling for a fight—but right now I feel like maybe the Freak isn't my enemy. Maybe it's just been trying to steer me right all along, show me a side of myself I couldn't see in front of Devon or Mark or maybe even Max.

I come out of the bathroom to look for Ash, and almost don't care who I stumble on—

But the first person I run into is totally unexpected, and when I hear that voice from behind me calling my name, it stops me in my tracks.

"*Dad?*" I say.

The Mom and Dad Show

"There you are!" says Dad. "Hey, Kim, I found him."

But Mom already sees me, I know—mostly because Mom is already running up with her arms out wide.

"We missed you, buddy!" she says. "We really missed you."

And all the anger goes out of me. I turn away for a second so they don't see the embarrassing sob I'm holding back. "Why are you here early? The showcase isn't til tomorrow." I don't give them a chance to answer before I go on: "Is something wrong? Do I have to go home immediately due to a family emergency?"

"Nice try, pal," says Mom.

"Didn't they tell you?" says Dad. "Tonight's the night we get to take you for dinner and hang out with you."

"They probably put it in a really long letter I didn't read," I mumble.

"Well, in any case, it appears you've been released on good behavior," says Mom.

"Oh, yeah?" I say.

"You sound surprised," Dad remarks with a glance. "Is there something we should know?"

"I'll tell you everything, but not until we're far, far away from here. Where are we going?"

"Okay, okay . . . we were thinking we *might* have seen an Indian place on the drive over," says Dad.

The Freak erupts with excitement. "*Indian?*"

"Oh, do you *like* Indian food?" says Mom.

"*I love Indian food*," the Freak tells them, like it is the very first time they have learned this fact.

But before we can get anywhere, I feel a hand on me and spin around out of nervous habit.

"It's the Harts!" Devon cheers, standing next to me with a toothy smile. He leaps into the middle of everything, just like always. "Don't worry, Mrs. Hart"—he grabs me around the shoulder and aims his smile at my mom—"I've been looking after this guy. We'll get him back home safe."

I feel a sudden heat burning down my back as I think about that confident arm around my shoulder. He keeps it there as Mom asks if he wants to join us for Indian food. I know it's Mom's way of saying sorry to me for being so suspicious of Devon when she dropped me off, but I can't possibly sit down and eat with him right now. All I can think about is watching him on the security camera video—his gleeful Cheesening.

"Mom, come on. Devon's going out with his parents tonight. Right, Devon?"

Devon doesn't really have time to react before I start pushing Mom and Dad toward the door. But Mom shoots me a stern look. She's not giving up that easy.

Please be good, Mom, I tell her with my brain.

Do you want Indian food or not, kid? she tells me with hers.

"Uh, yeah, my mom and dad are just running late. But have fun, you guys!" he says as we duck out the door. "See you when you get back."

"Count on it," I tell Devon.

The entire ride to the restaurant, Mom's trying to tell me what's been going on back home, but I barely hear it. I'm just replaying that video of Devon and Mark over and over again in my mind. If you could measure time in cosmo-flushes, it'd be an impressive number, but that's the problem with time machines: Keeping track of it all is really hard. Especially when you're inside of the thing.

When the car stops in front of the restaurant, the door swings open and this truly amazing smell smacks me in the face—and the joy of being here crashes over me with a wave all at once, like it's the very first time.

"I *love* Indian food," I say.

Why do I love Indian food, Tom? There's the smell, first of all. The heavy, thick smog of goodness that's hanging in the air from the moment you step in the door. And the sounds! Second of all are the sounds. Nobody's *ever* grumbling eating Indian food—everyone makes happy little "mmm" sounds until they turn into huge satisfied moans because they're so stuffed with good things.

Third through seventh of all are the big, round, soft pieces of naan I tear off. It's like having an entire loaf of bread to yourself, and a million things to dip it in. Chicken tikka masala, mushroom saag, mango chutney, and a whole bunch of other things I forget the name of—you've just got these huge heaping mounds of goo *everywhere*.

"They're not feeding our son, Kim," says Dad, somewhere between the fifth and sixth pieces of naan.

"They're feeding him," says Mom. "He's just stuffing his mouth full so he doesn't have to answer any of our questions."

"Is that right, Ian?"

My mouth is way too full to answer him.

"This is clearly a boy who hasn't seen food in weeks," says Dad. "And I for one am against an Evil Wacko Camp starving my child."

"It isn't Evil Wacko Camp!" I say, choking down the bread.

"It's not?" says Dad.

"No," says Mom, "it's a Wacko *Academy*."

"Mom!"

"A Wack-ademy," Dad fires back.

"Come on," I say. "We're not wackos, just normal kids who got into trouble."

Dad turns toward Mom and whispers loudly: "Wait, did he say he is a normal kid? Did we accidentally go to the wrong school?"

Mom makes a surprised face. "Oh, no!" she whispers back. "Is our real son still trapped at Evil Wacko Camp?"

"Maybe we should go rescue him," says Dad.

"Eh, we already ordered. Let's eat first."

I slump back in my chair with a hand over my eyes. "You guys. Do you *seriously* not understand why I have to join a gang of bullies to avoid getting beat up all the time?"

"Calm down and eat," says Dad. "We came to spend time with our son, not some impostor child."

"Can I have more naan, please?" I ask.

"You've had plenty, impostor child," says Mom.

"I don't want to *eat* it, I want to put it in my ears for earplugs so I can't hear you guys anymore."

Mom laughs. "Okay. This might actually be our kid."

But dinner's over way too fast. And when we're headed back to JANUS, the swirling mess that's waiting for me feels like it's twice as heavy as before.

"Hey listen," I tell Mom and Dad. "What if, instead of going back, we just . . . go home right now?"

Mom and Dad look at each other. "What about your friends?" says Mom.

"Mark and Devon can take care of themselves."

"And Ash?" she asks.

I feel a sideways lurch. She's right, I can't leave Ash.

"Yeah, I forgot," I say.

Stall Tactics

When I'm back inside, I make a point of avoiding all the places Devon might be waiting to talk to me. I just go right to the one spot where I can be alone.

I hold my breath until the door on my time machine is closed, but as soon as I exhale, a voice from the stall next to me pipes up:

"We need to talk, Ian," says Alva Anonymous. In the boys' bathroom.

I sit very still.

"Ian, you can't just ignore me."

"I'm not ignoring you, Alva."

"False," she says.

"Look, you're not allowed in here, and I'm kind of *busy* right now."

"And I'm not?" she asks.

"If you're so busy, why are you hanging out in the boys' bathroom and—were you *waiting* for me?"

"You've been hard to get to on your own," she says.

I sigh. "What do you want?"

"I need to talk to you. Was that not obvious?"

"No, I got it."

I can hear the door of her stall open and feel my teeth vibrate from the impact as it closes.

"Please come out," she says.

I know that time moves differently inside my time machine: Even though I'm not changing, the world around me is . . . and, what if, the next thing I know, Alva's gone! Disappeared forever? I better hurry if I want one last chance. Or so the Freak tells me.

"Hold on," I say.

I pretend like I'm actually using the toilet: With a flush and a huge Freakish smile, I open the door.

And there's Alva, arms folded. "Nice acting. I totally believed you were pooping, Ian."

"Ha ha ha," I say. Like, the actual words. Don't mistake it for a laugh. "Sometimes it's just nice to have the feeling of not wearing pants, ya know?"

She doesn't skip a beat. "So. It took me a while. But I finally figured out what's been going on with you and Ash."

As Alva looks at me and waits for my reaction, Cole Harper stumbles into the bathroom and gets his zipper halfway down before skidding to a stop face-to-face with Alva. He looks from her to me and back to her.

"No. Turn around," says Alva, pointing him toward the door.

"But I need to—"

"Bye bye," she says, shoving him into the hall.

And then Alva and I are just standing there. Staring at each other.

"So," she says. "Let's talk about your little *deal*."

"My little deal?" I ask her.

"Yeah. Mark told me all about the brilliant bargain you made with him. You know . . . the one where you and Ash promised to stop spending time with me and in return Miranda and Devon wouldn't try to get me *sent to the Village*?"

"Oh," I say. "Right." I make to go wash my hands.

"Yeah. *Oh right*." She pulls me back. "Is that really what Ash thinks of me? That I'm too weak to fight my own battles?"

"No, that isn't . . . we didn't mean—we were just trying to protect you, Alva."

She folds her arms.

"Ash didn't want to see you get hurt the way our friend Max did."

"I'm not some helpless little kid. And you aren't, either," she adds with a pointed look.

I swallow hard. "I know."

"And, honestly, I'm tired of treating you like one—even if you seem perfectly cool to let everyone else do it."

"I'm sorry we didn't tell you," I say.

"Me too, dude."

Before I know it, she's squeezing me in a tight hug.

"Is this some new form of argument that I don't understand?" I ask her.

By the way she laughs it feels like I did something right. I'm not totally sure what it is though.

"We're hugging it out, Ian."

"Oh."

"It was nice of you to be worried about me, I guess," she says. "Just don't ever do it again."

"It won't happen again," I tell her, which is a very meaningful promise, coming from a time traveler. Then something she said comes back to me: "Wait. Hold on. Did you say *Mark* told you about all this?"

She nods. "I guess he didn't realize how bad you guys would mope around. He thought maybe as long as the four of us kept hidden from Devon and Miranda . . ."

"Then we could still *secretly* get along?" I glance up at her, barely daring to believe.

"Having secrets is sort of cool," she says with a smile.

"It is," I agree.

Which is exactly why I decide to tell her about the video Jeremy showed me.

"Oh, man," she says after I explain. "Now I know why you're hiding in here."

"I may never leave."

"How's Ash?"

"Haven't told him yet."

She raises her eyebrows.

"I know . . ."

"Well?" She flicks her head to the door with a smile. "No time like the present."

Deep inside me, the Freak totally agrees.

Lights-Out

"**O**h man. Family is the *worst*, right?" Devon throws himself on his bed.

"Did something weird happen at your family dinner?" says Mark.

"Weird?" he says with bitter amusement. "Nope. Nothing out of the ordinary."

"LIGHTS OUT, BOYS!" the warning comes from the hall.

"Wait. Jeremy's not back," says Cole, looking at Jeremy's empty bunk.

"You think he got sent to the Village?" says Devon.

"No way," says Mark. "He's too smart to get sent there."

Ash and I exchange a glance across the room. We didn't get a chance to talk since he got back from dinner—because Devon wouldn't let me out of his sight—and now's not the safest time to tell him everything, not with all these bullies surrounding us.

Plus, the Freak won't shut up in my head long enough for me to think. It's *Devon* the Freak wants me to talk to now.

This is your chance to confront him, it urges. *He's messing with ASH!*

I look down at Devon, and the blood pumps in my ears.

Just say SOMETHING.

But my lungs won't fill. It's like gravity just quadrupled. Like a two-ton barbell is pressing down on me—

And then I see that I'm not at JANUS: I'm sitting in the cafeteria at East Huron Elementary School, and I'm chewing yet one more peanut butter sandwich in an endless stream of them.

As I take the last bite, I realize that it's not *Max* who is allergic to peanut butter . . . it's *me*.

It's always been me.

And I'm eating this sandwich—I just keep eating it, even though I shouldn't—and my airway is closing, and it's my own fault.

But the allergy attack feels like a jolt of electricity running through my bones and muscles. Preventing my brain from sending the message to *breathe*. My brain is shouting it over and over, but it sounds like a burbling creek's whisper and the electricity is a giant whitewater churn . . .

And I'm swept away.

For a minute, I can hear colors and the last day of elementary school is happening all over again but in reverse. And I come up with an amazing joke about how many Thomas Edisons it takes to screw in a lightbulb—but just when I'm about to tell it, my dog Scarlet rips past and steals my joke and gulps it down and runs away . . . and I'm chasing after her, and I'm stumbling right into the middle of JANUS orientation . . . and my uniform gets tighter and tighter and starts strangling me.

I know I'm having a nightmare—but I can't wake up; it's more real than being awake.

The more I fight, the worse it gets. Like quicksand. I wriggle and sink under the floor, and underneath is a murky, frigid river. I sink the whole way to the bottom—way, way down—and when I do, I find out I'm actually on my street in East Huron, only the air is replaced with water, and there's a boy in bronze clothing standing there right by my side.

Well, it's a statue of a boy, I guess. A twelve-year-old hero, preserved in metal and made into a monument of what all twelve-year-old boys should be.

Thomas Edison, you're such a jerk. A perfect, bronze little jerk.

The statue turns its head to look straight at me. "Come on, Ian," it says. And its voice is full of crackles, like a radio station that's not quite in tune. "I never claimed to be perfect."

That's what they taught us, though. You were awesome.

"Seriously, do you even know anything about me? I did some pretty bully-tastic stuff, and you'd know that if you bothered to look it up."

I haven't exactly had spare time, you know.

"You *have* had a lot churning around in your brain, I guess," says Edison. And as soon as he reminds me: *FLUSH*—we're back at JANUS, walking down an empty hallway.

"So what are you gonna do about Devon and everything, Ian?" Tom Edison asks me, and about five giant security cameras swing around and pin me in their unblinking gaze. Examining me. So I freeze, too scared I'll make the wrong choice. Because I don't want to be turned into a statue.

I'm not perfect, and I'm never going to be. I don't even want to be, I realize—and that's when I notice I'm not the only one being examined. JANUS is gone now, and I'm in a big, white doctor's office.

"There's nothing wrong with your son, Mr. Edison," says the doctor, tapping the statue of twelve-year-old Thomas Edison with a hollow, lifeless *Bong! Bong!* that vibrates along the floor.

"Then why does he think he's in the year two thousand and whatever, and he's stuck being some dumb kid's imaginary friend?" says Tom's dad. "Also why is he made out of metal? I'm pretty sure he wasn't always like that."

"Hmm," says the doctor. "Maybe we should pump him full of electricity and see if it helps."

"Is that really the best idea?" says Tom's dad.

"I dunno, but it sure sounds like fun," says the doctor, and when he smiles, I suddenly recognize that it's Devon—and then electricity screams through the young inventor's bronze body, and I'm ripped out of my dream and wake up shivering in my sweat-soaked pajamas.

The Two-Faced God of Bully School

"**Y**uck," I say, peeling back my sheets and feeling like I've been turned inside-out.

I look out the window for any hint of sun in the sky but it's way too early still.

"You okay, Ian?" Devon's voice floats up from below. "Sounds like a rough night up there."

"Yeah, weird dreams," I say.

"Least you can sleep," says Devon. "I can't sleep at all."

"Sorry," I say, though I'm not very.

I roll over toward the edge of the bed, where it's not soaked with sweat. And I see Devon down below. For a head-spinning second, it feels like the nightmare was real and I'm still in it.

But then I get ahold of myself and remember that I *can* breathe. I'm so relieved I feel like I can do anything.

"Hey, Devon, can I ask you something?" I hear myself say.

"I know what you're gonna say," he tells me after a pause.

"You do?"

"Come on, Ian, it's kinda obvious you're mad at me. Is this still about Alva? Because Mark's pretty sure *she's* the one who wrecked Ash's dad's book."

"Pretty sure she didn't," I say, the last of my hesitation falling away with his lie.

"You need to trust me that she's screwed up, okay? She's damaged. You don't see it, 'cause you *like* her, but eventually you're gonna thank me for keeping you from making a fool of yourself."

"You think I'm gonna *thank you*?"

"I know it," says Devon.

"For *keeping me* from making a fool of *myself*?" I'm getting a bit too loud for a room full of sleeping bullies now.

"Someday, Ian, when you see things better," Devon says, "when you understand the way things work in the real world—"

"In the *real world*"—I spit the words out like rotten food—"people who treat people the way *you* treat people don't get to keep their friends. You *have* to stop being a bully." A couple other kids stir under their blankets.

I feel the bunk shift as Devon shoots out of bed and gets right up in my face. "Oh, because you're such a good friend, Ian? The way I recall it, when Max had that accident, it was *your* peanut butter sandwich."

"Devon—"

"And you let *us* take all the blame. And we didn't give you a hard time at all, did we?"

"Dev—"

"And then you didn't talk to any of us for a week. Remember that?"

He pauses, and I keep quiet.

"And then everything this summer—all I've done to stand up for you—and still, *still* I'm not meeting your standards?"

In the back of my mind I'm vaguely aware that about half the dorm is now listening to every word.

"You know, would it really kill you to just be grateful, Ian?"

"*Grateful*? You think I'm not *grateful*?"

"Yes."

An unfamiliar heat sears through my neck, and I can feel it like a warm, red coal burning in the middle of my back. The place where the Freak calls home.

"Devon," I rumble. "I've tried *everything* to make excuses for all the horrible things you do. Because I convinced myself you were really, deep down, *good*."

He sneers back. "Seriously, Ian, how do you even survive being such a little baby? Oh right! Because I bail you out whenever you get in trouble."

"Yeah, all right. I'll admit it: You do bail me out, Dev. You're my friend. And if you'd just treat other people like you treat us, then *they'd* see you like *your friends* see you."

He pauses for a second, and just when I think I'm getting through, I hear two words come out of Devon's mouth that he's never said to me before: "You're right. I *am* treating you different than everybody else. And it should stop."

My smile vanishes before it reaches my lips.

"From now on, I'll treat you just like the rest of them, Hart." He starts to back away from my bunk.

"Hold on . . ." I say.

"That's what you wanted, isn't it?"

"Guys?" says Mark.

"Too late," says Devon. "We're finished—aren't we, Ian?"

"No, it's gonna be fine," says Mark. "We'll take care of this, right, Ian?"

"Time to pick sides, Mark," says Devon.

Mark looks really confused. "Ian, just apologize. Trust me, okay?"

"Trust you?" The words make me angry all over again. "*Trust* you? How's your big investigation going? Figure out who ruined Ash's book yet?"

I feel a wash of satisfaction as my words crash over him like a wave.

"Really thought you were better than that," I continue.

Mark stumbles for words that will fix this . . .

"Don't waste your breath," says Devon. "Ian Hart is beyond our help."

"Funny, I was thinking the same thing about you," I snap.

"Still the same old Ian," says Devon. "I should've listened to the other kids that day we met: You *are* a loser and a weirdo."

There's a sound very close to but not exactly like a wolverine gargling mouthwash, and I feel something pulling at my heart—but it stays put for the moment.

"Never thought I'd see the day I was *bored* by your insults, Crawford."

"Look, guys," says Mark, trying again. "We just have to make it through the next couple days and then it'll all get better when we're home again. Right?"

"*What*'ll be better, exactly?" says Devon. "I'll just spend the rest of my life keeping Ian from getting beat up when he says ridiculous, geeky stuff, like I always do. I'm so not interested. Why are we even friends?"

"I don't know, Dev," I say. "Why *are* we friends?"

As the words come out of my mouth, I suddenly feel dizzy. Maybe somewhere in the future, I'm in a bathroom right now, reliving this horrible moment.

FLUSH! I hear across the hall.

And then the door creaks open.

". . . guys?" says Ash. "What's goin' on?"

Hello from Freedom

Ash looks at us in confusion.

I try to open a psychic link with him and download everything that's just happened into his brain, but Mark steps in between us.

It's a well-known fact that psychic links only work if you have a direct line of sight to the other person.

Worse, Devon goes right over to Ash and pulls him into the corner to whisper his own version of what's going on.

"Ash, you gotta know something," I begin as I jump from the ladder.

But Mark grabs my arm when I try to wriggle past him and whispers into my ear, "Don't do anything you're gonna regret, Ian. Ash doesn't need to hear about . . . you know what."

"He doesn't need to know that you betrayed him?" I say. "That you—"

"Ian, listen to yourself. Is this really about Ash, or is it about *you?* What good will it do, telling him any of that? Do you *want* Ash to get hurt?"

I hesitate, starting to doubt myself.

"Let's just—we'll figure this out, okay?"

But as quick as the doubt bubbles up, I push it back down. "You're screwing with me, aren't you?" I ask.

"Ian, relax," says Mark. "Just think for a second."

"You are!" I say. "I've seen you guys do it a *million* times— stop being such a fake! I know you're better than that . . . *you're* the one who told Alva the truth."

"What are you talking about?"

"There's more to you than *this*," I say, ripping myself free.

"What're you doing, Ian?" Devon growls.

"Ash, it wasn't Alva," I say. "It was Devon and Mark. *They* put the cheese in your dad's book."

"See?" Devon says over me. "What'd I tell you? He's defected to her side. She has him brainwashed or mind controlled or something."

"It wasn't Alva," I repeat. "Every single slice was Devon. And Mark watched the whole thing happen. He was Devon's lookout so he wouldn't get caught."

Except that I don't say "caught." What I say is "cau-*ugh* . . ." and then trail off to a wheeze because all the air has been forced from my lungs.

Devon is shoving me up against the bunk, squeezing my ribs so hard that I can feel them creak. And when my tailbone hits the floor, I scream in silence, without the air to make a sound.

All around us, bullies look on in shock.

There's no air in the entire room. It's all been vented into outer space. And we're just floating, dead in orbit. And then: The silence is broken like an egg smashing against the sidewalk.

"GOOD MORNING, INMATES!" booms Jeremy's voice from everywhere and nowhere.

A mariachi band explodes through the speakers a second later, and the pressure on my chest relaxes as Devon swivels to find the source of the sound.

"HELLO FROM FREEDOM," Jeremy's voice comes through the loudspeakers above trumpets and violins and tiny guitars. "GREETINGS FROM THE GREAT WHITE NORTH!"

"Jeremy?" says Devon.

"THAT'S RIGHT, DEVON! I JUST WANTED TO DROP IN AND SAY HOW MUCH I APPRECIATE YOU ALL FOR BEING SO *FRIENDLY* THIS SUMMER."

From flat on my back I can see everyone cover their ears and look around in confused alarm. Kids from other rooms begin to spill out into the hall: Jeremy has commandeered the PA system for the entire school.

"YOU ALL DESERVE A BIG THANK YOU. I THOUGHT THIS WAS AN APPROPRIATE WAY TO SHOW MY FEELINGS FOR YOU GUYS."

Over the screech of the mariachi band, everyone moans like they're dying—except for me. Jeremy's wake-up call came in the nick of time to save my neck . . . and as I glance up at the video camera in the corner of the ceiling, I get this idea that his timing wasn't an accident.

"ENOUGH!" Judge Cressett booms, like thunder in the distance.

It rolls and rolls toward us, until it's right here coming from a man in the doorway.

"What is going on in here?"

"ALL HAIL JUDGE CRESSETT," says Jeremy.

A human hot-air balloon is filling up the door. Five foot four, both tall and wide, and possessing the unmistakable voice of Judge Cressett.

We blink in the Judge's direction. This horrible musky cologne is rapidly filling the room, and a few kids start to cough and rub their eyes like it stings.

Mr. Dunford is right behind him. "It's okay, Your Honor. Go back to sleep. I can handle this."

"Clearly not, Dunford. You've already let one of the children escape."

As Dunford raises both eyebrows, the Judge calls out to Jeremy, "You're in a lot of trouble, young man!"

"TELL ME ABOUT IT," says Jeremy. "I JUST SPENT LIKE TWO HOURS TRYING TO MAKE THIS TAKEDOWN VIDEO ABOUT YOUR STUPID

REFORM SCHOOL. AND NO MATTER HOW HARD I TRY, IT'S STILL *LAME*. IT'S LIKE, PICKING ON PEOPLE WAS NEVER HARD BEFORE . . . I BLAME YOU, DUNFORD."

"Really?" Dunford perks up at this. "Jeremy, that's one of the nicest things I've heard in a long time."

". . . IS IT?" Jeremy exclaims. "IT WASN'T SUPPOSED TO COME OUT SOUNDING NICE. WHAT IS WRONG WITH ME?"

"Jeremy," says Dunford over the mariachi band. "Come back and let's talk, okay?"

"Yes, young man! Come back and face the consequences!" threatens the Judge.

"We're all very concerned for you, Jeremy," adds Dunford. "Where are you right now?"

"I AM IN THE WALLS. I AM EVERYWHERE AND NOWHERE. AND I AM WATCHING . . ."

"Wait," says Mark. "How can he even hear us? Are there cameras in here?"

"WHY, YES," says Jeremy. "EVERYTHING YOU DO IS RECORDED, MARK. DIDN'T YOU KNOW THAT?"

"It was in your orientation packets," the Judge says in defeat. "You have to read your orientation packets."

Devon and Mark would've gotten *away* with the Cheesening if they'd read their orientation packets, the Freak tells me inside my head, as the mariachi band screeches to a halt outside it.

"IMPORTANT UPDATE!" Jeremy's voice returns. "ON BEHALF OF THE COLLECTIVE, I AM CONFISCATING ALL THIS SURVEILLANCE VIDEO YOU GUYS MADE. ENJOY THE SHOWCASE, GENTLEMEN. SMILE FOR THE CAMERAS . . ."

And with that, he's gone. Well, his voice is, anyway. For a second, we're all just looking around, waiting for an adult to say something.

"Ian, what're you doing on the floor?"

"Sorry, Mr. Dunford."

"You're required to sleep in your own bunk. Seriously, we go through a lot of trouble to put your name on it and everything." He shakes his head as he sweeps back out the door, leaving some of us to moan and rub our eyes and others to think about what we just did.

"If Jeremy were here, I'd kill him," Devon mutters.

"After he just confiscated the video of you beating me up?" I ask, picking myself off the floor. "Seems UNGRATEFUL to me."

For a second Devon looks like he's going to shove me back to the ground, but Mark pulls him away. "Hey, come on. He made his choice, Dev."

"Yeah, he did," says Devon. "Coming, Ash?"

Ash stays put as they head toward the door.

"Ash, come on," Devon presses. "What're you waiting for?"

"I think I'm waiting for something to make sense," says Ash. "You really did it, Dev?"

"Did what?"

"You sat there, and you unwrapped sixty-four slices of cheese, and you turned the pages, and—"

"Unbelievable," Devon cuts him off. "It's *that* easy for you to believe the worst about me? You don't need to see proof, you don't need to hear my side . . . just because *Ian says*—"

"Yes," says Ash, without waiting for him to finish. "Do you really have no clue? In all the time you've known him . . . you never understood how good a friend you had in Ian, did you?"

Ash gives me a little punch, and at the exact moment he makes contact I actually feel that throbbing in my chest explode and disappear—the Scotch tape that's been holding my insides inside comes away like stitches do and reveals that the hole my heart keeps falling out of is all skinned over.

It'll have a cool scar now, probably, and if you squint at it right, there'll be words spelled out in there, like *good friend* and stuff.

"C'mon, Ian," says Ash, pulling me past Devon and Mark before I can get too distracted.

I'm glad he keeps focused too, because as we turn to go I catch a hint of morning light finally coming through the window. Yellows and purples and greens and browns—

It's amazing.

Even the pinks.

Kinder and Kinder

Out in the hall, Ash's breathing gets a little heavier. "This has got to be a nightmare or something."

"All right, all right," I say. "Hang in there. Do you want the bad news, or the good news?"

He glances up. "Bad news first."

"Well, you're definitely awake," I say.

He nods, swallowing that. "Great. Really counting on this good news, Ian."

"Follow me," I say.

Even before we're in the dining hall, I see her. Alva Anonymous. She's sniffing like she's in a trance, following a trail of cinnamon sugar. "Is it me, or does it smell like doughnut holes in—oh. Hey, Ash."

She stops short.

"Monkey bread, guys!" says Mr. Dunford, coming up

behind us. He shows us a gooey little nugget of dough that sparkles with the promise of the world's biggest sugar rush.

"There's also a croaking bush!" says Dunford.

"A *what*?" I ask. I'm pretty sure he didn't say "croaking bush," but I have no clue what it really might've been.

"It's French for 'a thing that crunches in your mouth,'" he adds. "Very fancy. Not *technically* traditional."

"Show me to the baked goods, Mr. Dunford!" I pull him away from Ash and Alva.

"Twist my arm!" Dunford leads me toward a table sagging under the weight of the sticky, gooey glory he calls monkey bread. They come in big loaves and there's more stuff too—a Jenga tower made of tiny, round, crispy pastries, for one thing.

"That is a croaking bush!" says Dunford.

There is a label on it that says *croquembouche*. Weird.

I peel a nugget away from the monkey bread and shove it in my mouth. I've barely begun to chew before my jaws seal together like they're full of cement. Delicious, delicious cement.

You could tell me I'd die if I ate another piece and I'd definitely weigh the pros and cons first.

I let out a zombie-ish sound of amazement.

"I know, right?" says Dunford. "In the old days it was a tradition for one of the teachers to bring in treats on the day of a big show. Dr. Ginschlaugh made all this himself."

"Dr. *Ginschlaugh* made this?" I pry open my mouth and say.

"He's a good baker. You should try his pies."

"Wait. You were here when you were a kid too?" I ask Mr. Dunford. "Same as Ms. Fitz?"

He nods. "We like to come back, even though it's not like we remember it. There are still a few reasons we think this place is special."

Just then I hear a toilet flush, and then another one, and I turn to see Ash step back into the dining hall, followed by Alva. Both are having a hard time staying attached to the ground, they're so much lighter now than they were a minute ago.

"You okay, Ian?" says Mr. Dunford, noticing my distraction.

"He's great, Mr. Dunford," says Ash. "Ian is *great*."

Dunford gives me a thumbs-up and heads off, just in time for me to tell them about Ginschlaugh's baking.

"Being a baker is a very good cover story for a modern henchman," says Ash. "Do you think the *Judge* used to come here too?"

"No. Not the Judge," says Alva. "He's a KinderCorp guy. All they want is to turn this place into one big Children's Village."

"KinderCorp's the worst," says Ash.

Alva shrugs. "It wasn't always so bad, you know."

"Since when are you an expert?" says Ash.

"Well, back when my grandmother and grandfather ran KinderCorp—"

"Oh come on," says Ash. "Your grandparents did not run *KinderCorp*."

"Of course they didn't," she says. "It was called 'Kinder and Kinder' back then."

"What?" says Ash.

"'Cause my grandparents were named Mr. and Mrs. Kinder, dude. Also, it was a catering company."

"A *catering* company?" Ash narrows his eyes at her in suspicion.

"They were famous for their secret sweet-potato tot recipe," says Alva.

"You really expect us to swallow that?" says Ash. Then he laughs, because I point out exactly how many tots he *has* swallowed here at JANUS.

"One hour until showtime, guppies!" Ms. Fitz calls out.

"Kinder and Kinder . . ." Ash mutters, walking away.

"You *do* believe me, right?" Alva leans in to me as everyone starts filing out of the hall.

"Even if I didn't, I'd pretend to just because it's what *should* be the truth."

She grins. "I like the way you think, Hart."

34

The Showcase Must Go On

"Ladies and gentlemen, welcome to JANUS!" Judge Cressett's voice rumbles across the amphitheater on the hilltop. "At this time we would like to ask everyone to please turn off their cell phones. The show is about to begin."

I look out from behind the flat we built and take stock of the audience. The amphitheater is teeming with moms and dads and sisters and brothers—all here to observe what will surely be known as one of the Five Great Tragedies in the Life of Ian Ontario Hart.

"Well, boys?" says Devon, with his usual confidence. "Here it is."

"Is this it?" says Cole. "The end of our innocent youth?"

"After this we'll never be the same," adds Miranda.

"Definitely the end of any political ambitions I totally didn't have," says Mark.

Devon jolts me in the shoulder. "Ready to embarrass yourself, Hart?"

But Cole gives me an encouraging look. "Just keep your head up, man. We'll get through it."

At the end of the day, I guess Cole's kinda all right, you know? I mean: If Alva likes him, how terrible could he be? I look at Ash and catch him reading my mind.

"I'm glad you patched things up with Alva for us, by the way," he says, leaning in. "Forgot to thank you for that . . ."

"Wait, didn't she tell you?" I ask. "I didn't fix it—Mark did."

"Mark?"

"Places, boys!" Ms. Fitz says to Ash and me, pointing toward our separate marks on the stage.

"No partner, huh, Hart?" says Miranda.

That's when I remember that, in all the madness, Jeremy made his escape.

"All alone, how pitiful," says Devon from his place next to me.

But before he can enjoy my reaction, he's distracted by something in the audience and forgets all about me.

"There!" he whispers, grabbing Miranda's arm and pointing out into the crowd. "Holy crap. You see him? Right there . . ."

I follow his hand. "What, your brother?"

Devon looks up, and for a second he seems like he

desperately needs to talk to me—until he remembers our big fight. Then he turns his back and returns to Miranda. "That's my crazy brother Colin."

Miranda cranes around to get a better look. "Really?" she says. "How'd he get here? Didn't you say your mom and dad didn't come?"

I startle at this. "Devon, your parents didn't come? But I thought . . ."

Devon just acts like I don't exist. He doesn't even do me the courtesy of glaring. "He must've, like, hitchhiked or something," he says to Miranda.

"Crazy!" she responds. "You are so lucky to have a cool older brother."

"Yeah, not really. He's probably—crap, he must be here to get blackmail on me," says Devon. "To cancel out my blackmail on him!"

She raises her eyebrows. "You gotta admire that commitment."

"He's *committed*, all right." Devon starts backing away from the stage. "Can you see his cell phone? I can't tell. I gotta get out of this."

"Where do you think you're going?" Miranda demands. "I need my partner."

"I can't go out there, Miranda," says Devon. "I can't let Colin get video evidence of me dancing in a stupid play."

Miranda cocks her head to the side with a dangerous coolness. "But, Devon, then *I'll* look like an idiot out there . . . you don't want that, do you?" There's this hard look on her face, but Devon doesn't see it because he's just noticing the wall of clones that have closed off his escape route at the stairs leading off the stage.

"You don't understand," he says.

"Ninety seconds everyone!" Ms. Fitz calls out cheerfully, and disappears to the other side of the curtain.

Devon pales and looks around for help from the rest of our discipline.

Razan smiles like she's been waiting for this moment all summer. "You know something, Rembrandt?" she says. "There comes a special day in every bully's life . . ."

"You mean, when they realize there's always a bully who's bigger than them?" says Remy.

"No matter who you are," Razan goes on.

"Feels good to be retired, doesn't it?" says Rembrandt.

"I feel particularly good today."

They turn back to Devon and watch with such glee that it makes me a little uncomfortable.

I look out at Colin, and back at Devon. The only way for him to escape is right out onto the stage. And Devon sees me starting to doubt and aims his next plea at me—

"Ian, come on. I've *always* had your back . . . I've always looked out for my friends—you *know* that."

It makes me feel guilty, but I look him in the eye and shake my head. "You don't get to call me your friend anymore."

I hear a harsh shush from Ms. Fitz. "Everyone settle down! This isn't time to talk."

"They're all ganging up on me," Devon whines.

"We sure are, Ms. Fitz," Alva says. "We're ganging up on him to make him go out there and dance like he's *supposed* to."

Ms. Fitz gives us a warning look. "You all need to be quiet and focus on yourselves—and you're *all* going on stage. In *sixty* seconds."

My eyes dart back to Devon. He's starting to shiver a little, like I do when I'm really nervous. I've never seen him do that before. Never.

"It's just sad, isn't it?" mutters one of the clones.

"You know when you go to an animal shelter and there's that mean dog you know is never gonna find a forever home?" whispers another.

I get closer to Devon, right up next to him, before anyone notices I'm there.

"Ian, get me out—"

"Shut *up*."

"Ian . . . please."

I think of all the times he looked out for me. "Okay, Devon. I suppose I do owe you one last thing. If this is what you *really* want."

"It is. *Please*."

"Okay. Ready?"

"Ready for what?"

"Good." I straighten his collar, and dust off his shoulder. For a second I can see his expression go from desperate to hopeful to confused—and just as he starts to open his mouth again, I look him right in the eye and give Devon Crawford the last thing I owe him.

I push him off the stage.

He lands after a three-foot drop, right on the side of his ankle. Everyone watches—everyone but Ms. Fitz.

See? I'm learning too Tom.

"Whoa, are you all right?" I ask Devon.

For a second, Devon looks up in shock and attempts to lunge at me—but as he tries to get to his feet, he just falls down again.

This time he cries out and everyone hears him.

"Devon Crawford!" says Ms. Fitz. "What are you doing down there?"

Devon opens his mouth but before he can speak, I interrupt him: "I think he's hurt, Ms. Fitz. Twisted his ankle, looks like . . ."

I look right in his eyes again—and this time I can see them go clear in comprehension as our psychic link connects and he realizes what I did for him.

"It's really bad," he says. "I can't dance like this . . ."

Ms. Fitz is instantly suspicious. "Thirty seconds before the show, you twisted your ankle and can't go on?" As she climbs down and checks Devon's leg, she asks the rest of us, "Who saw what happened?"

Miranda takes a step forward and shakes her head. "I'm not sure *what* I saw," she says. "But it was *freaking hilarious*."

It makes me more than a little bit ashamed of myself, hearing her approval, but I keep it together.

"I'm *really* hurt, Ms. Fitz," says Devon.

"They're already playing the song," Razan warns.

"Tell them to vamp!" says Remy.

"They can't *vamp*, it's a recording!" says Razan. "Ms. Fitz, where's the remote?"

"I got it, I got it!" Remy hits the button on the remote and the music changes to an old man speaking in Russian. He hits it again and it gets louder. And louder. He looks around for Jeremy, but then remembers Jeremy's gone.

"Fixed it!" says Cole, just as the Russian man goes silent. "Oh wait, nope—broke it. *But it's off now!*"

At this point, the Rs start to look a little panicked.

"Well, this is very bad," says Razan.

"Can anyone play Beethoven's Seventh Symphony, by chance?" says Rembrandt.

Miranda's head snaps up. "The Allegretto?"

Everyone slowly turns to face her.

"Ms. Fitz, did I hear someone playing a piano before?"

"Uh, yeah. Down in the orchestra pit." Ms. Fitz points to

the small clearing in front of the stage and Miranda rushes down to take her seat at a little old piano.

"Ms. Fitz!" Razan hisses urgently. "Showtime! Now?"

"Just a second . . . All right, Devon. You're off the hook. But if I take you to the nurse and there's nothing wrong with you . . ."

"Oh, I promise there is *plenty* wrong with him," I say.

"Can you make it to the parking lot if I help you?" Ms. Fitz asks Devon. "Or would you prefer Dr. Ginschlaugh carry you?"

Before Devon can answer, a figure comes around the edge of the stage: Dr. Ginschlaugh. And there's a second person with him.

"*Colin!*" says Devon. "Ginschlaugh, did you set this up? Now it makes perfect sense."

Ginschlaugh gives Colin a look and nudges him forward.

"Devon?" he calls out. "You all right?"

"Twisted my ankle!" Devon calls back. "Sorry you came all this way and don't get to see a show . . ."

"Forget the show. Just stay put."

Devon looks up at his brother. "Come on," he says. "Don't act like you didn't come *just* to see me fail."

Colin nods. "Yeah, I guess I deserve that." He leans down and loops his arm under his brother. "I'll take care of him, Ms. Fitz."

"We've got you, Crawford," says Ginschlaugh, grabbing him under the other arm.

Mark and I exchange a look of surprise, but it's nothing compared to the confusion on Devon's face.

Did Colin come to cheer for Devon? I ask Mark with a glance. *Is Dr. Ginschlaugh somehow using his henchmen powers to bring the Crawford brothers back together?*

"Deal with your personal problems on your own time, Hart," says Razan. "It's showtime!"

Remy and Razan hustle us all back to our places.

"Wait! I still don't have a partner."

"Improvise!" says Rembrandt as he passes me in line and steps into the light of the stage.

"*What?*"

"Just remember what you learned and fake it!" he hisses. Then he and Razan kick off the show. And make it look like dancing is the most natural thing in the world.

Like it's so easy, just to be yourself.

All that movement. The two of them are out there sparkling, Tom. It's mesmerizing, watching them. Like watching a fire burn.

Then we're all on stage, and I throw myself into what we rehearsed, all on my own—I just sort of trust my body to know what it's supposed to do.

And for the first time in my life, I kind of *get* why people like this sort of thing. I'm just letting myself be completely free—I'm just *dancing*, Tom. I'm dancing like a flame does. And I catch Razan's eye and smile, waiting to see how impressed she is with my sudden improvement.

That's when I notice her expression. The absolute *horror* in her face.

Apparently I still can't dance, Tom.

But I keep going anyway, dancing like a fire does. Like a beautiful, beautiful garbage fire.

Personal Reflection

I look at the cinder-block wall by my head, but I don't bother counting the marks there. They're just little pieces of the past now, and the day is already sprinting off without me.

Outside in the sunshine, the air is different than it was in the early summer. It has that feeling that it'll always be like this, but something in the back of my head reminds me that late summer is when everything is holding its breath, and it's all gonna change pretty soon.

Sooner than later it'll be time to go back to real school again. In fact, I could've left a week ago, they told me. Something about KinderCorp ending the semester early . . .

I don't know—*somehow* this Canadian hacker collective got hold of the footage of our Parents' Weekend Showcase, and they made this super, *painfully* funny video, and it went viral, and a comedian in New York City did some big show about

JANUS, and KinderCorp, and the teachers and stuff . . . and anyway, long story short: Now KinderCorp is gone and this place is going back to being a school for musicians and artists and writers, and yeah, dancers too. Only, the people who get scholarships are going to still be like us. Normal kids who got into trouble. It's like my dad says: *The more things change, the more they stay insane.*

Whatever, there was a really long letter with all the details. You should just read that. Point is: I graduated from bully school so hard that after I was done, the bully school closed down entirely. That's the truth, you can google it.

"Whatcha readin'?" Alva asks as she sees me waiting for Ash on the curb.

I look up at her and block the sun with my hand. "It's this thing I've been writing."

She tilts her head to try to steal a peek. "What, for school?"

"Kinda," I say, slamming the book and jamming it into my bag.

"Oooh, is it private?"

"Yes."

"Is it about *me*?"

"*No*," I say lamely.

She sits down next to me and holds out her hand. "Let me see it."

"No way. Maybe someday. When I'm older."

"Am I even going to know you then?"

I shrug. "Can't tell the future, Alva."

"You're supposed to say 'Yeah, totally, we're gonna be friends forever and ever!'"

"Hey. Don't lie to a liar, right?"

She nods. "I respect that."

"But wouldn't it be awesome if we were?" I ask.

She doesn't answer right away. "Listen, I'm really not supposed to do this," she says. "You gotta promise me you won't ever repeat what I'm about to tell you, all right?"

"Why?"

She looks sideways at me. "Do you promise?"

"Alva—"

"Promise, Ian!"

"Okay, I *promise*! I will never tell a living soul."

She looks around carefully in all directions. And she whispers in my ear: "I'm a time traveler too."

For a second I get a tingle. And then it turns into a cold embarrassment as I realize:

"You read my thing!"

"I have no idea what you're talking about," she replies innocently. "I'm totally a time traveler. Just like you. I'm from the future, and I've come back to the past, and I'm here right now to tell you that you are way more important than Thomas Edison. You don't have to believe me—you just have to be yourself and someday you're gonna see I'm completely right."

I look at her—a long, hard look.

"What?" she asks.

"Even if you *are* telling the truth, which you're not—a true time traveler would *know* that telling me about my future would ruin it."

"Oh? Why's that?"

"Because now that I know about it, I'll act differently than I would've if you hadn't told me what happens to me in the end. It'll turn out different now."

She shrugs. "If that's how you want it."

"It's not how I *want* it. It's just the rules! That's how it works, when you know your future . . ."

"That's the rules, huh?"

"Yeah."

"Well," she says. "I was always taught that the reason I had to learn the rules was so I would understand *why* they exist, and how they could be broken."

"You can't break the laws of physics, Alva."

"We hardly even know what we can do," says Alva. "Maybe you only have that awesome future because I came back in time to right here and right now and 'broke the rules' to tell you that you are such a fantastic dude."

As I start to wonder, she shrugs and points at the book in my bag. "Anyway," she goes on, "isn't it weird that we call a book a volume?"

"Don't try to change the subject." But then I can't help thinking about it. "Wait—why is it weird?"

"Well, it's not weird, exactly," she says. "It's just: In math, *volume* is how you measure what's inside of an object."

I blink.

"You measure the length and the width and the height of the book, and you multiply them. That's how you measure the inside of a book, according to math."

I blink again. "That's a crazy way to measure what's inside of a book."

"I know."

"It's like—a freaking *ocean* in there."

She laughs at me getting worked up. "I *know*."

As I look up at her, something in Alva's smile cracks—a jagged opening that cuts through all the names and stories and everything else, to what's really underneath. In an instant, it's gone. But I saw it anyway.

"Guess there are rules we just don't understand," she says.

"Guess so," I agree.

She shoves her hands into the pockets of her hoodie. "Anyway. See ya 'round, Ontario."

"Count on it, Kinder. We'll start again next time."

She clears her throat. "Right where we left off, okay?"

"Deal."

I watch her go a few steps, and I can see her whole life

spread out as she crosses the parking lot. Maybe she's right. Maybe we are from the future. Looking back and feeling like it's all worth it. Looking forward and feeling like it's all gonna work out okay.

"What a freak," I say to myself.

And as I wait for Ash, I open the book again and fall deeply into the ocean inside.

AN INCOMPLETE LIST OF IMAGINARY FRIENDS

A brief and utterly unsatisfactory acknowledgment of some of Ian's imaginary friends who didn't appear in this novel:

Kelly Ashton, who is a brilliant editor. Ian wants to thank you for being his very real champion.

David Levithan, who gave Ian a chance to tell his story. Happily, it turns out David knew Ian could write a book all along. Probably because David is a time traveler.

Everyone at Scholastic who made it possible for Ian to focus on telling his story, and for other kids to connect with him. He knows he's lucky to be in your hands. Specific thanks to production editors Rebekah Wallin, Cheryl Weisman, and Rachel Gluckstern, and to Yaffa Jaskoll for the book's wonderful cover design.

All the people Ian doesn't even know he owes, big time. Peter Ackerman, Sarah Rees Brennan, Barry Goldblatt, Michelle Hodkin, Dan Dunford, Sarah Nolen, Dan Poblocki, Tricia Ready, Colleen AF Venable: Thank you for your advice and companionship this past year. You've made this experience the best sort of adventure for a first-timer like me. Libba Bray, I am especially grateful for your wisdom and friendship in the writing trenches.

To my friends and family, who have been amazingly supportive, and especially my parents, Leann and Buzz Weinberger: I hope seeing this book become real feels at least half as good for you as it does for me.

About the Author

JUSTIN WEINBERGER has never been shipped off to bully reform school, but he still owes his sister an apology for hogging the Nintendo. Today, Justin works on TV dramas in New York City and lives in Brooklyn. *Reformed* is his first novel.